TWISTED
Colleen Snyder

FRIDAY

"So, what do you think?"

Walker kneeled in the ruined church, staring at the burn marks on the floor. She traced the patterns with her hand. Lifted her fingers to her nose and sniffed. Strode around the remains of the sanctuary, eyeing the charred studs. After a moment, she glanced at Pastor Mars. "This wasn't from a lightning strike. This was arson."

Wait for it. Wait for it. Watch his eyes.

Pastor Mars' eyes widened, then returned to normal. His cheeks reddened. His hands twitched. He grasped them and held them at his waist. He stammered, then pulled himself together. "Why would you say such a thing? How can you know?"

The voices in her head joined Pastor Mars in his accusation. *Yeah, how? You're an eighteen-year-old girl. You don't know anything.*

You're trying to get attention. Showing off. As always.

Did you really believe he wanted to know what you thought when he asked you? You have any idea what the term "rhetorical question" means?

Walker pointed out the signs. "The fire started in four different spots. You can see the burn patterns on the floor. I can smell the accelerant." She pointed to the walls. "All these caught at once." She stared hard at the middle-aged man. "You should call someone to investigate it."

Mars pulled his suitcoat into place. He settled his shoulders. Raised his head. "I'll call the fire department. The chief can make the determination if he thinks there's enough evidence." He stared at Ron Jennings, the leader of the relief group. "Does this mean you won't start the teardown? That's what you came for, isn't it? To help us rebuild?"

Ron shook his head. "We'll have to wait for the fire chief." He nodded to Walker. "She's got the good eye. Also, the background." He smiled at her. "Such as it is."

Walker didn't smile back. *Thanks to you, Robert Winger, I have myriad skills. None of which I ever wanted. But it wasn't a choice you gave me. You taught me how to lie, cheat, steal, hide my crimes...do anything and everything to make a dollar for the company.*

Ron tried to be diplomatic. "Once we get the okay, we'll tear this thing down in a day. In the meantime, I'm sure there are other places we can be of service. But yes, that is why we came. To help this town rebuild."

Excellent use of your psychology schooling, Ron.

The category three tornado, which tore through Rallins, Indiana, devastated the farming community. From the rise where the small country church stood, Walker could see a row of houses without roofs. Trees lay across porches. One old oak had smashed through a garage door. Another had been uprooted and dropped into a front room. Bushes, tree limbs, and debris from homes littered the streets. Those were only the houses she could see.

Walker hiked back to the army barracks tent in the field behind the church. It sat below the hill where the church had stood. Mars apologized profusely for the accommodations or lack thereof. With the devastation in the little town, the congregation had nowhere to put the relief team from Oakton, the capital of Ohio. Cots were set up with a canvas curtain to divide the men's living quarters from the women's.

Her twenty-five college mates sat on top of and at the four

picnic tables provided for their use. Ten women, plus Walker, thirteen men, plus Ron Jennings, made up the all-volunteer team. Walker, the youngest, Ron, the oldest. He'd delayed his college career two years before starting a major in Psychology. Now in his fourth year, he was the "old man" of the team at twenty-four. Everyone else fit in between.

Racially, they were more diverse. Like the Sunday school song sang, "Red and yellow, black and white," plus every hue in between. Ron's dark skin contrasted with Walker's pale white Anglo-Saxon background. Two of the women were of Latino descent. Jun hailed from India. Benjamin came from Israel. Maybe they weren't quite "every tongue, tribe, and nation," but they were close. Their most common denominator was they'd all been homeless.

Walker slipped into the table where the females sat. Maria, with dark hair, beautiful eyes, and perfect complexion, glared at her in mock anger. "What did you say? Pastor Mars looked happy until you started talking."

"He asked me what I thought about the condition of the church. I told him it burned because of arson."

Maria sighed. "Of course, you did. He responded how?"

Walker stared at the table. "How could I possibly know? I'm a kid. What would I know?" She didn't bother keeping the bitterness from her voice.

"Is that what he said? Or how you interpreted it?" Maria's voice lilted in jest.

Ignore her. She doesn't know you. No one takes you seriously. You are loved.

Ignore Him. He doesn't know you.

Walker repeated the pastor's words verbatim. "'How can you know?' I'm a kid."

Maria's eyes twinkled. "Maybe if you let your hair grow long instead of practically shaving it, maybe if you wore a little make-up, maybe chose some decent shoes instead of those high-tops, people wouldn't assume you're a kid. They'd recognize you for the sophomore in college you are. Even if you are only eighteen."

Walker breathed slowly. Maria tapped the table lightly. "Passing as a boy worked for you on the streets, Walker. I understand. I do. But you've been off the streets for two years now. Think about putting it away. You have a new life. You're a new creation. Appreciate it."

Walker lowered her eyes, staring at the ground. Anger rose in her memory. She closed her eyes. "I wore make-up. Lots of it. Short dresses. High heels. My handlers made sure I appeared 'of age.' I swore I'd never again let anyone make me pretend to be what I'm not. Not even myself." She stared up into her friend's eyes. "God may forget my past, but I can't. There are too many reminders."

She chewed her lip as the anger faded as swiftly as it came. There were other memories, though. Walker admitted, "We're in Indiana. He told me if I ever set foot in this state again, I'd be found and killed." Walker snorted. "Not something you forget."

Maria shifted on the bench. "Does he still have power over you?" The woman held Walker in her gaze. There was challenge in her eyes. Gentle challenge, but still demanding a reckoning.

"I'm here, aren't I? I came on this trip. No, he doesn't hold power over me. But so many seeds were planted in my life..." Walker trailed off. She shook her head. Raised her eyebrows. "I'm a work in progress which may never be done."

Maria smiled. "We're all works in progress, Walker. We can only live it one day at a time." She shifted around to see what the others were doing.

From the men's table, Jun, the math major from India, yelled, "Hey, Walker. Get your basketball. Let's play."

Before Walker could rise, Ron rejoined them. "I talked with Pastor Mars. Since we can't start on the church, we can go door-to-door to ask people if they want help. Some might be waiting for their insurance companies to come out. Some could be ready and would love the muscle. We'll start in the morning. Everyone down with that?"

Twenty-four heads nodded. Jun pointed to Walker but directed his question to Ron. "We're going to get a game going. You want to play?"

Ron shrugged. "Why not?" He looked back up the hill. "I don't think the pastor can see us enough to object to a co-ed competition."

Jun chuckled. "Especially since it will be twenty-four against one." He grinned at Walker. "But you will still beat us."

Walker shook her head in mock anger. "No, I won't. I'm a team player."

Maria laughed. "Yeah. She's on the girls' team. Five on five. With her, we will beat you."

Walker ignored the trash talk and hustled to her bunk. She retrieved her ball from under the cot. The feel of the hard rubber stilled her soul. Her love, her passion. She only felt fully alive on the court. Pine floor or asphalt, it didn't matter. She could be herself. It was the only time the inner voices were silenced.

The young people moved to the mostly abandoned basketball court. There were hoops but no nets. Free throw lines remained in evidence, but the center line had been scuffed out. Sidelines were non-existent. Contrary to Maria's claims, the teams were split three-two, men to women. Maria threw the ball up. Play began.

Walker's mind went into game mode. Nothing existed except the ball, the basket, and the players in between. Run, run, run. Pass. Run. Pass. Block. Shoot. Pass. Block. Run. Run. Run. Shoot.

She had no idea of the score, who was ahead, or by how much. If there were observers, she didn't see them. Nothing mattered but the precise movement of the ball to the goal. Her passes sang. Her shots dived through the hoop. Her blocks were clean with passion. Walker lived and breathed on the court for the love of the game.

Only when someone—Ron, maybe?—called, "Game!" did she return to awareness of the world around her. Everyone breathed hard, hands on their knees, bent over double to catch oxygen for their lungs. Adrenaline surged through Walker. Her face hurt from smiling. She glanced from player to player. "Who won?" She bounced the ball in front of her.

Maria gasped, "Do you really care?" Her hair, wet from sweat, plastered itself against her forehead.

Walker grinned. "No. Did we play a good game?" She picked up her dribbling and held the ball.

Ron slung his arm around her shoulders and squeezed. "Yes, yes, we did."

Walker froze. Life drained from her, sucked into a black hole in her being. Her eyes lost focus. Nightmare memories engulfed her. She stood stock still, twitching almost imperceptibly as remembered blows assailed her body. Again. Again. Again….

A voice broke into the emptiness. Gentle. Quiet. Soothing. "Walker. Walker. You're okay. Listen to me. Listen to my voice. You're here at the church. You're with friends. Your brothers and sisters in the Lord. We're all here for you. You're in an illusion. It's past. It's gone. Over. Done. Not real. You're safe. You're loved. Come back, Walker."

The sound reached into the desolation. Seeped through the walls. Became light in the blackness. A trail to follow out of the long ago back to the now. Walker's eyes closed. She took a deep breath, let it out slowly, then opened her eyes.

Maria stood in front of her, eyeing her closely. "Are you with us?"

Walker nodded. She bit the inside of her mouth. Her classmates stood in a semi-circle around her, watching, waiting for some sign, some signal she was okay. She smiled and ducked her head to the side. "Kinda lost it there."

Jun snorted. "I guess so."

Ron's face had paled. "I'm sorry, Walker. I didn't know. I…"

Walker interrupted his apologies. "Stop. I didn't know, either." She shook her head. "Fight or flight. My brain went to flight. Nothing to fight with." She took a deep breath. "It's over now. I'm back. I'm fine. I still want to know how the game went."

Jun laughed. "You don't know? Your team won, of course."

His eyes sparkled. "You even switched sides for a bit to help us out, but it wasn't enough."

Walker stepped back. "I what?" She glanced from player to player. No. She wouldn't do it. Not knowingly. Consciously.

Ron laughed as well. "Yeah. You told me you wanted it not to be a blowout, so you swapped sides midway through the last quarter. Made it close, I'll tell you that."

Walker snapped a look at Maria. "I did what?"

Maria grinned and pointed at Jun. "What he said. You did. You don't remember?"

Walker shook her head. "I don't remember anything when I'm playing. It's all a blur."

"So were you. Woman, you play the meanest game of roundball I've ever seen. Why aren't you on the team at college?" The group drifted back to the tent area.

Walker's joy drained from her. She shrugged. "Too busy. Work. School. Volunteering. I don't have time for sports."

Jun nodded. "When we are in Brother Matt's work-for-college program, there is not a lot of free time." He stretched his arms over his head.

Walker added, "If I were majoring in sports, it would be different. My major is social work. That way, I can be useful when I'm done."

Maria eyed her. "You're useful now, Walker. God is using you in everything you do."

Using you? You're worthless. No one needs you.

I don't know. She's good for a laugh ever so often.

Yeah, when she tries to do something intelligent. That's always hilarious.

Walker bowed her head slightly. She trailed her demons back to the tent. Reality returned.

~

Later in the afternoon, Walker saw Pastor Mars approaching

the tent. He had a tall man in a white shirt, blue slacks, and a black-billed hat with him. Maria sat beside Walker at the picnic table. "Seems like the pastor found the fire chief."

The two men came to the table. Pastor Mars nodded to Walker and Maria. "Miss. Miss." He motioned to the man beside him. "This is Chief Zachary. I told him what you said about the fire. He'd like you to show him what you found."

Zachary extended his hand to Walker. "Miss."

"Walker. No miss. Just Walker." She stood, returned the handshake, then led the men to the burned-out shell of the church. She pointed out the evidence she'd seen. "The burn marks are off." She pointed to the shadows on the floor. "You can see the fire started in several different places. Lightning doesn't do that." Walker motioned to the floor. "I smelled an accelerant. Possibly kerosene, but I'm not sure." She indicated the studs. "There's too much damage for a fire that burned in a thunderstorm. The rain should have extinguished more of it." She stepped back, watching Zachary.

The fire chief walked around the room, examining the areas Walker pointed out. After a moment, he stared at her. His eyes narrowed. "Where did you learn all this?"

"I'm trained to observe." She gave them nothing else. *Let's not admit you were taught to set fires. How not to make it appear like you had.*

Yeah, they don't need to know that part of your history.

Or any other part of it, either.

Zachary nodded. "You did it well." He turned to Pastor Mars. "She's right. She nailed it. Shame. You might have been able to rebuild the kitchen and narthex. It wouldn't match the old structure. But now you'll have to rebuild the whole church."

Mars shook his head. "Yes, it's a great pity." His cheeks reddened. He lowered his eyes. He stepped back to be behind Zachary. Out of sight.

Zachary eyed Walker. "Don't suppose you'd be interested in joining the department, would you?" The smile read as genuine.

Walker shook her head. "No, sir. I'm studying social work."

Zachary motioned down the hill at the team. "Your group. You're going to be here for what, a week?" He leaned forward on one foot.

"Possibly longer, sir. We're prepared to stay as long as we're needed." She shrugged. "Or until spring break is over. We've all got studies to resume."

The fire chief nodded. "You think I could entice you to work for me while you're here?"

"Doing what, sir?" Her gut tightened. *"Entice." Bad word.*

Stay in the now. Walker focused on the fire chief's face. Watch the eyes.

"Examining the other houses with fire damage. Our arson investigator works for the county. He's tied up in Bell. He may not get back for a week or more. I could use your powers of observation"—he smiled—"to check out places around here." He shook his head. "I don't expect you to find anything, but it won't hurt to put eyes on the worst places." He held out his hand. "What do you say?"

He's genuine. The eyes don't lie. Walker still hesitated. "I'd need to discuss it with my team lead, Ron Jennings. If he allows it, I'll work for you." She dredged up a smile.

Zachary pulled a card out of his top pocket. "This has my number. Call me after you've talked to him. Tell him I could use you." He smiled. "Might be easier than swinging a hammer."

Walker chuckled. "Agreed, sir. I'll talk to him now." *Breathe. It's all good.*

"Excellent." The man put his hand on her shoulder and squeezed it. "Thank you, Walker."

Walker's eyes focused, unfocused, focused back. *Do not stiffen. Do not react. Nod. Walk away. Do it. Do it.*

I am with you.

Walk away, now.

Walker nodded. She moved down the hill. Closed her eyes,

blanked her mind. *No flashbacks. No flashbacks. Stay in the now. Stay connected. Stay…*

Voices screamed in her mind. She shut them out. *Step. Step. Step. One step at a time. You can do this. You can do this.*

Walker reached the tent. She sank down at the table, laid her hands on the top, gripping the rough wood. Beside her, Maria intoned, "The Lord is my rock and my fortress. The Lord is my strong tower. I run to Him and am safe."

Walker breathed slowly, dropped her shoulders, opened her eyes. She gave Maria a wane smile. "Thanks."

Maria ducked her head to the side. "I saw him. You did good."

Walker chuckled. "Yeah, I didn't deck him." She scrunched her shoulders to her ears, then dropped them again.

"You didn't freak out, either. You're making progress." Maria smiled.

Walker breathed in slowly. "I suppose. Have you seen Ron?"

"I think he's over at the barbeque pit, figuring out what's for dinner." Maria pointed across the hill.

Walker glanced over to the cook area. Members of the congregation who still had houses to live in had set up a large pit, two flattop grills, plus several prep stations for meals for the group. Smells of meat grilling wafted from the makeshift kitchen. Two generators powered refrigerator/freezer combinations. The team was well-supplied with food and drink as a thank-you for their efforts.

Walker and Maria drifted over to the area to join their team. Ron looked at Walker. "Hey. Saw the fire chief with Pastor Mars. What did he say?"

"He wants me to work with him for the next few days. Check out some of the houses with burn damage to see if I think there's any chance of arson. If there is, they'll have to wait to start until the actual investigators come. If not, we can begin the teardown."

Ron held up his hand. "High five! Nice work."

Walker returned the high-five but shrugged. "He's short-handed. He'll take any help he can get."

Ron eyed her sideways. "Admit you did good. Your powers of observation are needed. You've been chosen to do something important. You're not bragging. You're admitting someone finds you of value. Accept it, be glad of it, and move on. Got it?"

Walker rolled her eyes. "I hear you."

"But do you believe me?" Ron's eyes narrowed as he waited for her response.

Walker chewed the inside of her cheek. "I'll work on it."

"I guess that's as good as it gets, right?" Ron chuckled.

"For now." She pointed to the pit. "What are they cooking?"

"Pig."

Walker's head snapped up sharply. "What about Ben?" Benjamin, who laughingly called himself the "token Jew," walked up to join the observers at the pit.

He grinned at her and jumped into the conversation. "I received a special dispensation from Brother Golding. He assured me God would forgive me for not eating kosher while I'm here." He chuckled. "I'm not sure my mom will, but God will." He peered around to see who might be listening. "I haven't told her I haven't eaten kosher since I got to school. It will break her heart."

"I'm sorry, Ben." What would it feel like to have convictions you had to break to help others?

You only need one conviction. Do what I tell you to do. Always. Without question. Hear me, girl?

Ben laughed. "I'm not. Gentiles eat all the good stuff."

Smells from the kitchen drifted over the fields. Ron's eyes narrowed as he surveyed the amount and variety of food being prepared. He tapped one of the cooks on the sleeve. "This isn't all for us, is it? I mean, we're college kids, but even we can't eat all this."

The woman smiled. "No. Pastor Mars told us to expect a crowd. Your team gets to eat first, then any neighbors who are doing without can join you."

Ron frowned. "They shouldn't have to wait on us. We can all line up together."

The middle-aged woman shook her head. Her face bore the lines and creases of loving on people and laughing at life. "No, dear. I know the neighbors. If you want food, you best eat first. Trust me. Dinner will be at six for you, six-thirty for the rest." She patted Ron on the shoulder.

Ron chuckled. "I'll take your word for it." He walked back to the table to wait for the dinner bell.

Ten minutes later, people began drifting in down the hill. Many carried chairs. Some carried children. Some had baskets, threw down blankets, set out plates and silverware. Farmers still in their overalls gathered with wives and children. Mothers corralled small people. Baseballs were thrown around. To Walker, it seemed like a TV network definition of a town picnic. *Is this what 'home' is?*

You'll never know.

In Me, you are home.

Except someone is missing. You'll never be home.

A literal bell rang. "Dinner's on. Come and get it." None of the newcomers rose or made a move to get in line. Ron waved to the team to gather round. He lowered his voice so only they could hear. "The sooner we get through the line, the sooner these people can eat. Keep them in mind when you load your plates." He raised his head. "Let's pray."

Ron offered thanks for the food and the hands preparing it. The team broke and lined up.

Pork, fried chicken, baked beans, green beans, something a server identified as "collards" (Walker passed on those), coleslaw, cornbread, biscuits… Walker took a small sampling of everything (except the greens). She found a place to sit away from the crowd. Ron passed by and ordered, "Up. Go, find a family to sit with. We're visitors and strangers here. Make friends. Meet new people. Extend the love of the Lord to someone."

Walker scowled but rose to obey. She picked out a woman by

herself (if a woman with three children can be called "by herself") and asked, "May I join you?"

The woman smiled. "Oh, thank you. Please. Sit."

She had laid out a checkered blanket which two children crawled all over. The third child was older. Walker guessed a girl, maybe four. The two toddlers were around two, maybe younger. Walker sat. "Hi. I'm Walker. Nice to meet you."

"Cheryl." The woman pointed to the children. "This is Louis, this is Franny, and this is Melody."

Walker smiled at the older child. "Melody. That's a beautiful name."

The little girl ducked her head. "It's my grandma's name. She gave it to me."

"It's very pretty."

Cheryl looked around, then asked, "May I ask you a huge favor? Would you stay with the children while I get them their plates?"

Do not react. Do not panic. Smile. Say, "Of course." You can handle small children.

Since when? I don't know nothin' 'bout handlin' babies!

Smile. Say, "Of course."

Walker smiled. "Of course. I'd be happy to help."

Liar.

Shut up.

Cheryl stood and took Melody with her to the serving line. Walker set her plate behind her, eyeing the little ones. They both stared at her, stared after their mother, then stared at Walker. She smiled brightly. "Hi! Want to play a game?"

The youngest's lower lip started to tremble. Walker grabbed her biscuit. "Here!" She split it between the two toddlers.

Her action won her a stay of execution. The babies crumbled the biscuits in their hands. They dropped the crumbs in their laps. They mashed the crumbs into balls and stuffed the balls into their mouths. Which made more crumbs to gather into balls. By the time

Cheryl returned, the biscuit had become sand on the blanket.

Cheryl asked, "Were they okay?" She set two plates on the blanket. Melody set her plate down, shooed her brother away from it, then sat to eat.

Walker smiled. "They were just fine." *I survived. The biscuit didn't.*

Cheryl gave the littles a piece of ham to chew on. "What made you come here?"

"Brother Golding, the pastor at the street mission we go to, knows Pastor Mars. Pastor Mars asked for help. Brother Golding recruited us, so we came."

"That is sweet of you. Your team is so wonderful for coming here to help us out."

Walker admitted, "We're all indebted to Brother Golding. Not one of us would deny him anything he asks. We all owe him everything."

"He must be a special man." She chewed her food, then spooned slaw into the younger children's mouths.

"He is." *I owe him my life. If he hadn't pulled me off the streets… Of course, we're all his rescues. Which is why we won't tell him "no."* Warmth trickled into her being. Was she feeling love for the man?

Love is earned. You must reach my perfect standards to get it. Which I change to suit my whims. You will never, ever be good enough to earn love. Not mine, not anyone else's. Never. Walker lifted her head and returned to the present.

Cheryl made small talk about the area until the children lost interest in the food. They decided crawling all over the adults would be more fun. Walker endured being used as a climbing tower. She breathed slow. *These are children. Babies. They will not harm you. They are not your father. They are not your marks. They are not your handler. They are babies.*

The taunts in her mind didn't help. It never did.

You can't do this. You're going to freak out.

Walker's gonna panic. Wait for it…
Peace I give you.
She can't do this. She'll never make it.

Walker smiled through gritted teeth. She could feel her hands twitching, but no one else would notice. She would suffer through it.

After probably an hour of torture, Cheryl decided to take her munchkins home. The woman gathered her blanket, gathered her babies, and left. Walker closed her eyes. She drew in deep breaths through her nose, letting them out slowly. She relaxed her shoulders inch by inch. Calmed her trembling hands.

Maria slid over beside her. "I am so sorry. I saw you over here but couldn't get away from the couple I sat with. They wanted to give me moment-by-moment details of their trauma in the tornado." She groaned. "Moment-by-moment. Every last second."

Walker stretched her neck. "It's okay. I survived." She dropped her shoulders. Looked at Maria. "I survived. I didn't zone out, I didn't hit back, I didn't scream. I survived." She smiled.

Maria grinned. "You're doing it, Walker. You're making it through it. Brother Matt knew you could. That's why he included you on this trip."

Walker grumbled, "Yeah, well, he and I are going to have a discussion about what he 'knows' versus what I know."

"You'll lose." Maria laughed. Her eyes twinkled.

"I know I will. But we're still going to talk about it." Walker picked up her plate and stood.

Maria directed, "Come on. Ron says he wants to do devotions so we can get to bed early. I think he's got a worksite in mind for tomorrow. We'll need our rest. Or so he says."

Walker nodded. "It's what we're here for." She grinned. "I'm going to need the exercise if I keep eating like I did tonight." She tossed her plate in the trash receptacle.

Maria laughed. "You and me both, Walker. You and me both."

The women walked back to their tent.

~

A burst of profanity exploded in his ear. Greg Willis waited until it subsided. "Is there a question in there?"

The caller seethed, "Who torched the church?"

Greg remained calm. He straightened his suit jacket. "No one I know."

"Yeah? So why is Zachary searching for arson?"

Greg glanced out the window of his office. The second-floor view was blurred by the broken glass yet to be replaced. Otherwise, he'd be seeing the town square. With its obelisk smashed against the cannon. Centuries-old maple trees pulled up by the roots and dropped in the mini-mart's front door. Rebuilding this place would take years.

He returned to the conversation. "He received a tip from an anonymous source. One of the college bunch who came from Oakton. Some young woman in the group knows about arson."

"I am ordering you to keep them away from the Maugham house. Do you hear me?"

Greg's jaw tightened. "What would you suggest I do? I can't order a tornado at will." What did he expect?

"No, but you can ensure a house falls on our witch. Send her back to Oakton. In a coffin, if you have to."

Greg's voice became still. "Don't you think five deaths in this town are enough?"

"What do you want me to say?" the caller sneered. "You have your orders. Do it."

The call disconnected. Greg ground his teeth and shoved the phone into his pocket. He stared out the window. Emptiness filled him.

Greg pulled the phone out, scrolled through his contacts. "Trip. Listen, the boys are on break this week. I need a favor. Yes, one of those favors. I need some of the boys to join the relief team from Oakton. Right." He waited. "I don't care who you send. Right.

There's a girl they need to keep occupied. Personal favor. She needs to be kept away from the Maugham's house. Yeah. I'll explain why after the Oakton team is gone. Until then, keep her busy. Good."

He returned his phone to his pocket. Greg's eyes stared back out the window. *Five deaths. That was not supposed to happen. Not the whole family.* His hands trembled. He was in too deep to back out, though. Right? No, he hadn't held the torch. But had he lit the flame? He looked out the window. No answers. He sighed and resumed his paperwork.

SATURDAY

Walker dropped her load of twisted lumber into the wheelbarrow and went back for another. She saw a group of five burly muscle-bound young men approaching the site her group had worked on all morning. The newcomers might be college-age, late teens, maybe early twenties. They carried themselves like school athletes. They had a determination in their steps. An almost harmony in their walk. Like they were a team. *Basketball team. All the starters, I'd bet.*

If you had anything to bet with. Which you don't.

You could bet your reputation. If you had one.

Walker ignored the inner insults and concentrated on her work. She gathered another armload of debris, then headed back to the wheelbarrow.

One of the newcomers caught up to her. He held out his arms. "Here, let me take your load."

"There's plenty more to pick up." She motioned to the demolished home. "If you're here to help, check in with Ron. The one in the Ohio State University Buckeye shirt. He'll give you a section to clear."

She noted his eyes flared as the young man observed who she meant. *Not used to a person of color in charge? Welcome to the new world.*

The man shrugged. He extended his hand. "I'm Bobby."

She gave him a nod. "Walker. You still need to check in."

Walker moved past the man to continue working. *Work. Work harder. You never work hard enough. You're lazy. You're useless. You're....*

The litany continued. Always. Walker dumped her load, went back for another. She saw Bobby and his team approach Ron. She continued gathering debris but watched to see what the newcomers would do. Ron pointed out positions for them. Discussions followed. Ron pointed again. Negotiations. Ron shrugged. The new team dispersed. Walker's eyes narrowed as she saw the men conveniently pair off with the women. *Surprise, surprise.* Bobby headed over to rejoin her.

He smiled. "Lucky you. I'm your assigned mule."

Walker gave him a tight-lipped smile. "Prepare to work." She loaded him with as much splintered lumber as he could carry, loaded her own arms with an equal amount, then marched to the collection site. When they reached and dumped their loads, Walker directed Bobby, "You don't have to wait for me. Go get another load."

Bobby grinned. "You do like to give orders, don't you?"

Walker raised her eyebrows. "Are you here to work? Work." She banged her gloved hands together to knock off the soot.

"Why so unfriendly? We want to help." Bobby's face smiled. His eyes…his eyes.

Walker pointed to the five homes—or their remains—along what had been a quiet street. "Help is welcome. When the street is cleared, and these homes are ready for rebuilding, we'll make nice and be friends. Until then, I'm working." She brushed past him to return to her gathering.

She worked another hour before more intruders arrived. Walker raised her head and saw Fire Chief Zachary approaching. He looked around the clean-up area as if searching for someone. He caught Walker's eye, then made a line for her. Walker pulled herself inward.

Zachary smiled. "Walker! There you are. Hey, Bobby. When did you get here?"

Bobby dropped his load to shake hands with the fire inspector. "About an hour ago. Team's on break for the week, so we decided to come help out." He jerked his head toward Walker. "I got the strong, silent one." Again, the smile. Again, the eyes didn't.

"You got the smart one." Chief Zachary smiled at Walker. "My new assistant." He handed her a bundle of red and green flags on metal sticks. He instructed her, "If you find anything suspicious, tag it for further inspection. If you don't, leave a green one. I'll know it's been checked."

Walker met his gaze. "I can't promise I'll get them all correct."

"You caught the first one. Arsonists don't usually stop with one when there are so many available. All I'm asking is for you to try. Can you do that?" He waited for her answer.

Walker nodded. "Yes, sir. I'll do what I can."

For what that's worth. Which ain't much.

Chief Zachary squeezed her shoulder. "That's what I wanted to hear."

Walker froze. *Move. Breathe. No flight. No fight. Breathe. Do not panic. Do not respond. Breathe.*

The chief smiled at Bobby. "I like this woman. She knows how to work hard, she respects her elders, and she takes responsibility. You should find a woman like this, Bobby. She'd be a keeper."

He let go of her shoulder. Walker let out a silent breath. She relaxed her shoulders. Exited vigilant mode. Stayed in the now.

Bobby shrugged. He chuckled. "I want one who will talk to me, too."

Zachary laughed. "I'm sure Walker will talk when she gets to know you." He smiled at her. "Call me if you need anything."

The chief reached out to shake Walker's hand. She pulled off her glove, stuck it in her back pocket, then returned the handshake. Chief Zachary turned, got back in his car, and drove off.

Walker pulled her glove out of her jeans. The ash smudged her backside. The rest of her would be the same shade of gray by day's end. Walker grabbed another armful of rubbish, carried it to the pile, then looked around for Ron. Her team lead whacked at broken two-by-fours, bringing down a leaning garage. Walker headed to his position.

Bobby trailed behind her. She ignored him. "Ron, I've got to leave for a while. Chief Zachary…"

Ron cut in. "I know." He set his sledge down, surveyed the area. "Maria!"

The third-year pre-med student set down her axe. She glanced up from her pile of lumber. "What?"

Ron motioned with his head. "Will you go with Walker to examine some of the burned houses? I don't want her going alone."

Bobby raised his hand. "I'll go with her." Walker mistrusted his enthusiasm.

Ron waved him off. "We don't send men and women out alone." He smiled. "Prevents problems. Or perceived problems." *Thank you, Ron. Thank you, Brother Golding.*

Bobby laughed. "I'm harmless. Honest." He waved his hand to give a dramatic bow.

Ron shrugged. "Doesn't matter. We still don't send a guy and a girl out alone." He eyed Maria. "Will you?"

Maria dusted off her arms. "Yeah, I'll go." She straightened her back stiffly. "It'll be nice to stand upright for a little bit." She smiled at Walker.

Ron chuckled. "Lucky you." He held Walker's eyes. "Be careful. No heroics. Check with me when you get back."

What worried him? Walker assured him, "I will." She turned to Maria. "Ready to go?"

Her teammate nodded. "Yeah. Let's do this."

The two women walked down the street. Bobby trailed a step behind them. Walker rolled her eyes at his company but said nothing. Maria grinned. "Can I get an introduction?"

Walker jerked her head to the young man. "Bobby. I don't know his last name." Maria nodded to him. Walker continued her introduction. "Maria Williams. She's a pre-med major." Walker's eyes glinted. "Don't fall down, or she'll practice on you."

Maria bumped Walker from the side. "I only did that once. The guy wasn't moving."

"He was sleeping off a bender. Really surprised him when you started CPR."

Maria laughed. Walker chuckled. Bobby's eyes widened. "She does talk!"

She never stops talking. Her mouth runs non-stop. All of its garbage. She doesn't know anything. She's useless. Walker kept walking.

The group reached the first house with fire damage. A tree had fallen on the porch, the windows and doors were missing. Part of the roof had been blown off. Walker examined what she could see of the structure. Fire marks moved down the remains of the roof, radiating from a hole the size of a small car. Walker checked the gutters. Two were melted at the ends. She nodded to Maria. "Lightning strike. This one's okay." She planted a green flag in the front yard close to the street. Anyone driving by could see it and know to keep moving.

Maria didn't ask questions. Bobby did. "How do you know?"

Walker pointed to the top of the structure. "You can see where it hit. Blew a hole through the roof. Walked down the gutters to melt the ends."

She moved to the two-story house across the street. The roof remained intact, but the rest of the house was missing. Studs still anchored the upper third of the second floor. Maria eyed the building. "It's not safe to go in." She pushed against a beam. Part of the ceiling collapsed.

Walker nodded. "I'm going around the back. I want to look at the kitchen."

The three walked around and peered in the shattered window. Fire had gutted the wall behind the stove, which lay under the dishwasher. Walker leaned sideways to try to get the best angle she could.

Go in. You won't know if you don't.
Stay out where it's safe.
You're a coward. Go in.

Walker bowed her head, letting the two sides battle it out. After a moment, she lifted her chin. "It started in here. I'd say not arson. Let's move on." Accusations of *Coward!* followed her to the street. She planted the green flag. The group moved on.

They searched three more houses with fire damage. All appeared to be from natural causes. Bobby stretched after the third house. "This is pointless. There's no arson out here. Only the church got hit."

Walker ignored him. She headed down the street. Maria followed her but asked, "What do you think?" Was she siding with Bobby?

Walker continued, more determined. "I think I need to check the rest of the houses. There are a couple more on the next street, then one on the cul-de-sac on the way back." She eyed Bobby. "If you're tired, go back. No one said you had to make this trip."

Bobby turned to Maria. "Is she always this anti-social?" His eyes narrowed, but he smiled. Always smiling.

Maria shrugged. "Ask her yourself." She picked up a broken stick and swung it along as she walked. She hummed a praise chorus. Content. Maria exuded contentment. Very little rattled her. These days.

Bobby raised his eyebrows at Walker. "Are you always this anti-social?" His eyes issued the challenge.

"When I have a job to do, yes. Zachary asked me to check the homes, so I'm checking the homes. I'll be social when we're done." Walker didn't look at the young man. She dismissed him as either ally or friend. Baggage. He was baggage.

"Why can't you do both?" Bobby stepped closer to Walker.

"Because it takes my mind off the focus of the job. Work is work. Rest is rest." Walker left it there. Work mattered. Work gave you value. Earned you… Nothing. In the end, nothing.

Maria chimed in. "Except you never rest, Walker. I've seen you. You're in school all day or at the rec center tutoring. Nights, you're studying. Weekends, you're back at the rec center coaching basketball. Sundays, you're helping set up for church." Her voice softened. "Helpful is one thing. Driven is something else. Who drives you?" She held Walker's eyes. "Don't say it's the Lord. He gives His children rest." She stopped and stood in the center of the sidewalk. There would have to be a reckoning.

Walker lowered her eyes. After a few moments, she admitted, "It's ingrained in me. Pounded in me. Work. Work hard. Rest when you're done."

Maria's voice softened even more. "But you're never done, are you?"

Walker partially sucked in her bottom lip. Her eyes lost focus…no, they focused on a time and place in a past not so far removed. She stared off into the emptiness. "No. I'm not."

Maria held out her hand. "May I?"

Walker hesitated. Hesitated. Hesitated. She nodded. Maria put her arm around Walker's shoulders. Walker leaned into the comfort and warmth. They were a sensation she wanted to get used to. If they weren't so scary. So vulnerable.

Bobby chuckled, interrupting the fragile moment. "That's why you don't like me. You like girls better." He grinned. "Nothing wrong with that. You could have told me up front."

Walker glared at him. "I don't like 'girls better.' I'm not interested in a relationship with anyone right now." She shrugged at Maria. "Maria knows. My life is complicated. Maybe when I get it sorted out, I'll feel different."

But you'll never get it sorted out. This is you for the rest of your days.

You are a new creation.

Not you. Never you. Not with your past.

Maria's eyes glowed. "You're doing a good job, Walker. Considering where you were, you're doing good."

Walker shook her head. "The Lord is doing good in me. I'm along for the ride." Considering where she came from, only the Lord could do any good.

Maria prodded a little deeper. "But you had to be willing to go with Him. Which you are. So, give yourself credit for saying 'yes.' It's what He wants to hear, anyhow."

Credit? Credit? You don't deserve credit. You owe me for everything, including your sad existence. Credit? I'll show you credit.

Walker snapped out of the memory, losing the comforting moment. Her face darkened. She stiffened under Maria's arm. Her teammate lifted her arm from her shoulder and stepped away from her side. Walker swallowed hard. She stalked to the next house with fire damage.

They checked two more houses. One to go. Walker motioned down the street. "We have the one on the cul-de-sac, after which we're done on this side of town. I'll get the north side tomorrow."

Bobby stopped in the center of the street. "Listen."

Walker and Maria stood still. Walker narrowed her focus to catch any sound.

Nothing.

She stared at Bobby. "What did you hear?"

"It sounded like a cry." He pointed to a house supported by one pillar with a tree leaning against the side. The rest crumpled into a pile of rubble. "There."

His eyes twitched side to side. Barely. *Careful. Careful. It's a trap. He didn't hear anything.*

Never trust anyone. Especially a man. They always want something.

Walker shook herself mentally. She stepped around the carnage but stayed out from under the leaning mass.

Bobby's eyes opened wider. "There it is again." His eyes twitched again.

Maria and Walker exchanged glances. Walker heard nothing.

She stepped closer to the wreckage. Walker started pulling boards from the pile. She pointed to Maria. "Check around the other side. See if there is anywhere big enough for us to get through to the inside."

Maria hustled to examine the back of the house. Bobby pulled out twisted boards, throwing them into the yard. The pile groaned and shifted. Walker held up her hand. "Stop. Just stop. Wait. You'll bring this whole place down." She eyed the mound of debris like a pile of pick-up sticks. One supported another supported another…pull the first, pull the second….

She pointed to a half-burned board. "That one. Get that one." Bobby wrestled six feet of board from the pile. Walker reached for the one under his. One plank at a time. Working together, they pulled a small hill of lumber clear of the mass. The opening exposed more of the insides of the house. Walker kneeled and called, "Can anyone hear me?"

No answer. Walker pointed out another board to Bobby. "There. Get that one." He pulled. She pulled. More of the opening showed. She called another time. "Can anyone hear me? Is anyone there?"

A muffled, anguished voice rasped, "Help."

Bobby's eyes flared wide. Walker noted. *You didn't expect to get a response, did you? You didn't hear anything before. You intended this to be a trap.* Walker pointed out more boards. Bobby shook his head. "It'll collapse." Fear flooded his voice.

"Let it. We have to get them out." Walker started shifting the wood, trying to make the opening larger. As she strained against the lumber, tree limbs settled further on top of the pile. There would be no entry here.

Maria returned. "There's an opening from the kitchen. I don't know how far down it goes." Her face bore concern.

Walker pointed to the hollow. "There's someone alive in there. I heard them." She called, "We're coming to get you. Hang on. Just hang on." *I have to save them. I have to. It's up to me. That's why*

I'm here, right, Lord? That's why You put me on the team. To save this person. I have to get them out.

They ran around the back. Maria motioned to a small hole under the floor, possibly leading to the cellar. "It's all I could find. I don't know...."

Walker took one glance. "I'm smallest. I'm going in." She didn't allow time for debate but slipped in feet first before Maria could say no. Walker wiggled to make it through, scraping her sides going in. But she would not quit.

You'll quit. You always quit. It gets hard, and you...

Walker seethed, "Shut up! I'm not quitting. I'm getting them out." She closed her eyes. "Lord, You brought me here. Show me where to go, what to do. I can't do this alone. You have to show me how to reach them. Please. Take my life, but save them."

The cellar was dark, half full of furniture. Wreckage from the levels above had fallen through the missing floorboards. Walker made her way around what she could, over what she couldn't. Water dripped from the ceiling. Light seeped in around the damage, giving Walker enough illumination to make her way to the front of the house. She came up behind the pile of destruction. She called, "Talk to me. Where are you?"

The voice whispered, "Here. Over here."

Walker spun around. A dresser hung from the first floor. A mattress and box spring were twisted into pretzel shapes. "Where? Where?"

"Here."

Walker slung anything and everything in her path. Nothing mattered but getting to the voice. Nothing. *Hurry. Hurry. Hurry. Now.*

She yanked at the last of the rubble in her way. Under a tool bench, trapped by a table saw, lay a young woman. She cuddled an object in her arms. Walker pulled, lifted, lifted, pulled...and moved the saw by inches. She screamed, "Lord! Help me!"

The saw moved again. Walker jerked at the tabletop, mindless of the blade which whipped across her arm. It didn't matter. Nothing mattered. The victim mattered. "I'm getting it. I'm getting it." She heaved one last time. The weight shifted. The woman rolled away from the bench, gasping and groaning in pain. Walker carefully pulled her from the hole she'd sheltered in. The bundle moved. An infant.

The woman passed it to her. "Help her."

Collin's eyes flared wide. She cradled it the way she'd seen the mother do. Held it. Gazed into the face, the eyes. Lay the child beside her mother.

"Weak. I'm so weak." The woman's eyes blinked rapidly. She coughed and moaned. "I had some food…dried fruit…granola bars." She pointed to the open ceiling. "Rainwater puddled enough to keep me going until yesterday." The woman coughed, then hugged the child to her side. "I breastfed the baby. But without water, I'm getting dry, and she can't get enough to eat."

Walker whipped her head around the room. No way could Walker lift the woman out how Walker had come in. Somehow, they would have to pull her from the open end.

"Maria!" She yelled it as loud as she could. "Maria!"

Bobby's voice came back. "She's gone for help. I hope she makes it."

Could you put some enthusiasm into it? Some hope? Some conviction? "Keep pulling those boards. But be careful. There's a dresser hanging. I don't want it to fall. Seems stable enough right now, but I don't want to take chances."

"I'll do what I can." Silence followed.

Walker rubbed the woman's arms. "What's your name?" Talk. *Talking means you're alive. Keep talking.*

"Alissa."

"That's pretty. What's the baby's name?"

"Katrina."

"I like it. It's nice. How long have you been down here?" *Stupid question. Since the storm, idiot.*

The woman shifted on the floor. She stared into the baby's face. "Last Friday. When the storm hit." Her voice shook. "They say shelter in the basement. Always in the basement. No one tells you what to do when the house collapses on you."

"No, they don't. Do you live here alone?" Were there others to rescue? Would there be bodies she needed to find? Would they be in one piece? How bad would it be?

Alissa hugged her child. "Katrina and me. And our dog." She tried to laugh but coughed instead.

Walker looked around the cellar. "Is it down here, too?"

"No. He got out the first night." Alissa shook her head. "I half expected him to bring help, you know? 'Timmy's in the well. Go get help, Lassie.' But he didn't come back."

Smart dog. Walker asked, "Where are you hurt?" *How do I keep them alive until help comes?*

"My leg is numb. My shoulder hurts. My chest hurts." Alissa closed her eyes. She sobbed. "I thought we were going to die here. No one heard us. I called and called, but no one answered."

Walker turned Alissa's leg so she could examine the wound. She yelled over her shoulder. "Bobby! How's it coming?"

No answer. No sounds at all. *Is he gone?*

Walker pulled off her shirt, ripped the arms out, then wrapped them around the woman's leg. It wasn't bleeding, but it would be once they started moving her. "Is Katrina hurt?"

"No. I sheltered her. I couldn't let my baby die. I couldn't. All I care about is keeping her alive."

Alissa coughed again. Walker stood. She moved to the kitchen end of the house where she'd crawled in. Maybe she could shimmy up and get water? Or maybe…

Walker examined the pipes in the cellar. One of the copper ones had a spigot. She had to yank on it to open it, but water trickled out. Fearful it would run out too soon, Walker soaked the rest of her shirt. She moved back beside Alissa. "My shirt's clean. Sort of. Wipe your mouth with this. Suck on it. It'll get you some water, anyhow."

Alissa followed the instructions. The woman sucked as much moisture as possible from the threads. Walker squeezed water from the hem into the baby's mouth. The little one moved her lips in response. "How old is she?"

"Three months." Short answers meant Alissa hurt too much to chatter. Her voice grew weaker.

Walker paced the cellar, then went to the open end. She called up. "Bobby? You up there?"

No answer. She turned away. Sounds of wood shifting position spun her back around. The dresser swayed. The motion threatened to bring it down on Alissa and the baby. Walker grabbed a board to try to push the drawers. She yelled, "Bobby! Stop! Wait!" No answer. More boards shifted. The dresser trembled. Walker shoved as hard as she could to move the dresser's trajectory so the rear would come down further away from the victims.

The board wasn't strong enough. Plan B. Walker reached as high as she could, barely high enough to touch the end of the bureau. If she could break its fall… It slid from its perch. Walker shoved with everything she had and shifted the angle enough…barely enough…maybe enough…

The dresser broke free of its hold. It crashed down on top of Walker, missing the woman and baby. Walker took the brunt of the load on her back. Her head smashed into the cellar floor. But the rest of her stayed on her knees, bowing under the weight but not flattened.

No sound came from her lips. *You don't cry. You never cry. Hear me? Never. I don't care what hurts. I don't care how much it hurts. You do not cry, ever. Got it? No? Cry about this. There. Want to cry some more? Yes? Feel this.*

Walker swallowed all the pain. She would not cry. He would not win. Never again. He would not triumph over her. Her left wrist collapsed. *Broken. Again.*

Alissa screamed. "Are you okay? Are you okay?"

Walker gathered control of her voice. "I'm fine." She rolled out from under the dresser, then leaned against it. "Not my smartest move, but I'm fine." She sat still to gain her breath. Assessing the damage to her body would wait. *Alissa and the baby still need to be rescued.*

Alissa wept. "You saved us. Twice, now. You saved us. Oh, thank you, Lord."

"Amen." *Thank You, Lord. You saved them. Get them out of this basement, please. Alive.*

Walker heard sirens in the distance. Closer, she heard Bobby yelling, "Walker? Are you okay? The dresser fell." Boards shifted over her head, dropping dirt and tree roots on her.

Walker dropped her head back against the furniture. "Really? I had no idea." She leaned forward to get volume in her voice. "Where have you been?"

"Pulling boards, like you said. The rescue squad is on the way. You hear them?"

What game are you playing? Why? She would need to find out. As soon as Alissa and Katrina were safe. "Throw me your shirt."

"Why?" Such indignation. Really? Over a shirt?

"Because I need it. Do it." The shirt rocketed down between the boards. Walker caught it. She pulled it over her head. It covered the scrapes and cuts nicely. *Hidden. Good.*

A gentle nudge of disapproval at her action disturbed her. She acknowledged it reluctantly. *I'll tell Ron when we get back. I promise. But first, Alissa gets taken care of. My injuries don't matter.*

It took another hour before the rescue squad, accompanied by the fire department and half the able-bodied residents of the town, were able to shift the wreckage enough to get the victims. Walker refused to leave the cellar until Alissa and the baby were lifted out. Only after they were safe did she accept the rope hoist, which brought her into the harsh searchlights turning the neighborhood from night to day.

The crowd cheered as Alissa and Katrina appeared. Walker

closed her eyes. Could she sneak out some other way? Some way she wouldn't be seen or recognized? Disappear into the night with no fanfare?

Nope. As the rescuers lifted her from the cellar, another cheer broke out. She recognized the camera lights of the local news network. *Great.*

Panic filled her. What if he saw? What if he recognized? She grabbed a hat from the first body she could see, then pulled it low over her eyes. With the dirt and sweat, no one should know who she was. *Please, God. Please. Protect me. Please.*

Paramedics cleaned and bandaged her wounds. The nurse who dressed her arm motioned to the waiting ambulance. "Do you want to take a ride to the hospital? They can check you for any other injuries."

Walker hesitated. A trip to the hospital would get her away from reporters. But a trip to the hospital could bring up questions she didn't want to answer. Like, "Why do you have so many broken bones? Where did all these scars come from?" No, she'd face the reporters. She had an idea of how to deal with them.

As she cleared the triage area, a news anchor rushed up. He shoved a microphone in her face. "We want to hear it from you. How did you find Ms. Hicock? What were you doing out here?"

Walker peered desperately for Ron in the crowd. She spotted him behind the rope barrier the police had set up. Walker stuttered severely, as if unable to speak, then signed her answer in American Sign Language. The newsman backed up slightly. "Someone get a translator here."

Walker ducked away from the reporter. She ran to Ron. She grabbed him around his middle and whispered savagely, "Hide me." She signed, "*Sign with me.*"

Ron's eyes widened, then narrowed. He signed, "*What's wrong?*" He held up her arm to check the bandages, shook his head, dropped her arm.

Walker responded, "*I can't be seen on camera. No one can*

recognize me or hear my voice. Help me."

The reporter, joined by others, reversed field and came rushing to Ron's position. He held up his hands. "Please. Please. She's been through a lot. Let her have some peace." He semi-sheltered Walker away from the cameras.

The newsman complained, "We just want to ask her some questions. Only a couple."

Ron tipped his head. He signed, *"It will make them go away faster."*

Walker shook her head. Ron signed again. *"Give them two questions. Three at most. It'll get it over, and we can get back to the camp."*

Walker glared at him. *"I hate when you're right. Okay. Two questions. And stay in front of me."*

Ron glared at the crowd of reporters. "She says only two or three. She wants to go back to the church to rest."

"How did she find Ms. Hicock?"

"We were examining the damaged areas. Bobby heard a sound, so we investigated. I crawled into the cellar and found her."

"Weren't you afraid you'd be trapped or killed down there with them?"

"The Lord watched over us. I knew He was with me."

The newsman hesitated. "Pastor Mars says your name is Walker. You're studying social work. Are you…"

Fire Chief Zachary burst into the interview. "Let's give Ms. Walker some space to breathe, okay? Give her a chance to get cleaned up. You can make arrangements to talk to her tomorrow or the next day. The main thing is Alissa and little Katrina are safe. Ms. Walker is a hero; we're all grateful for her."

He moved between the cameras, microphones, and Ron, blocking Walker from sight. He raised his eyebrows at Ron. "Sign language?"

Ron directed Walker away from the crowd. They walked toward the church bus. Zachary waited until Ron, the rest of the college group, and Walker were all on board, then climbed in after them. Walker looked down the aisles for Bobby or his team. They were nowhere in evidence. She sighed.

Ron slid into the driver's seat. He started the bus. He asked the question no one had asked yet, "You hurt bad?"

"I'm never hurt. I don't hurt."

He revised the question. "You injured anywhere?"

"Scraped, bruised." She did not mention the wrist. She would bind it herself, then tell him she'd twisted it. No doctors. There would be no doctors. Ever.

Zachary asked, "Why the ruse back there? Just didn't want to answer questions?"

Walker eyed Ron, then turned to Zachary. "You trust me. I trust you. One of the basketball team members who came down to help followed us. When Maria went for help, he stayed behind. I told him to pull boards to help us escape, but I never heard anything moving. A dresser which hung in place for over a week decided to fall on us."

Zachary's eyes narrowed. "Are you blaming Bobby?"

Walker repeated, "I'm saying he was with us, then he wasn't. After the dresser fell, he was suddenly back again. I don't know what's happening. Maybe I'm just paranoid. I'd like to talk to him before I draw any conclusions."

Zachary fell silent. After a moment, he asked, "Did he know you were checking out the burn patterns?" He stopped. "Of course, he did. He was there when I talked to you this morning." He fell silent again. "Seems almost strange the team would show up today after all the time that's passed. They never offered to help before."

He stared in Walker's eyes. "I don't know what is going on, either. But I won't say anything if you don't want me to." He chuckled. "I won't tell the channel seven crew you can talk."

Walker nodded to him. "Thank you, sir. There is one more thing you can do for me. Make sure there were no pictures taken of me. If there were, they aren't to be released on any public forum."

He smiled. "You aren't wanted now, are you?"

Walker snorted. "Nobody wants me. The Lord is stuck with me, but He's the only One." She hesitated. "There is one man who might still be very interested in knowing where I am. I'd like not to cross his path."

"Who would he be?"

Walker stared at the floor. "A man named Robert Winger." The name made her shudder on the inside. Never on the outside. Never show. Never tell.

"Who is he?"

Walker didn't lift her eyes. Her face held no expression. The shell returned. "My biological father." She turned and stared out the window at the darkness.

SUNDAY

Morning brought Walker to her feet. Everything ached. Every muscle in her body resisted the idea of getting off the cot. She ignored the pain. Mind over matter. Move. Keep moving. *You're lazy, that's all. You don't want to move. You can if you want it bad enough. You just don't want to.*

Ron yelled over the divider, "Walker. You're excused for the day. Stay here."

Walker dressed and went out. She waited until Ron appeared to confront him. "I'm fine. I can work."

"Maybe you can. But you're not going to. I have to answer to Brother Matt when I get back about the shape of my team. I don't want him thinking I didn't take good care of you. I'm doing this for my benefit, not yours. Live with it."

Walker scowled. He grinned, then walked to the cook area. "Who wants eggs?"

~

Walker watched her teammates drive off to continue teardowns of the damaged houses. She scowled, frowned, and kicked at a tuft of grass. "I'm fine. There's nothing swrong with me. I can work."

You're pretending to be hurt. You're always pretending to be hurt. You're lazy...

Walker silenced the voice. "I am not lazy. I didn't choose to stay here. I was ordered to stay."

She sat on top of the picnic table, staring at the town. There was one house she could examine…the one in the cul-de-sac she hadn't visited yesterday. Maybe she could walk over there and check it out. She wouldn't be working…the walk would ease the protesting muscles. Maybe…

Walker went into the tent and came back with her Bible. Maybe she should start the day in the Word first. There was so much she didn't know about the Savior she'd pledged her life to. Brother Matt assured her He loved her. He'd accepted her as she was. Flawed, scarred, damaged, guilty. He'd washed her clean, made her a new creation. But where would she find the proof? How did she know?

"It's all in here," he'd told her, holding the Bible. "You have to read it for yourself. Read it. Get it deep down inside you. Live it every moment of every day. Live it like your life depends on it. Because it does. For you—for us—it does. It's our life, our hope. Streets are tough. Jesus is tougher."

Walker opened her Bible.

She read for an hour. She read until her eyes grew tired and the words jumbled on the page. Time to stop.

Walker put her Bible away. She retrieved her basketball. She stepped out on the court to begin working. The wrist complained about being used. She ignored it. Pain meant nothing. She ran baseline to baseline, dribbling. She practiced her free throws until she could consistently nail ten in a row. Dribbling behind the back. Between the legs. Side to side. Every movement deliberate, controlled, polished. Over and over.

She finished her repetitions when she heard voices laughing. She looked up the hill to see Bobby, with two teammates sitting on the grass, watching her.

Walker recognized the redhead as Larl. The dark-haired young man had been introduced the day before as Virgil. Virgil commented, "Not bad."

Larl asked, "The girl or the work?"

Bobby sneered, "Has to be the work. The girl is ugly as a mud fence."

Oh, is the mask off now? I survived your little trap, so it's full-on nasty? Give it your best shot.

Virgil elbowed his teammate. "Shut up, Robert. She's not." The men moved down the hill and approached Walker.

Give them nothing. Ice. You're strong. You're…

I am with you always.

You can take them. All of them. All at once. Do it. As soon as they get close.

Walker slowed her dribble. "If you came to help, the team is over on Windrow Street."

Virgil nodded. "Thanks. Guess we're a little late."

"Ron likes to start early. Gets more work done that way."

Larl motioned for Walker to throw him the ball. "Pretty good ball handling for a girl. Want to see how it's really done?"

Virgil shoved him. "You got nothing on her. Shut up, man."

Walker tossed the ball to Larl. "I can learn from anyone. Show me."

Larl laughed. "No, I'm joking. You're impressive. I haven't seen that kind of ball movement since Coach Newell."

He passed the ball back to her. Walker hesitated, her brain moving a thousand miles an hour. *They're a team. I could learn.*

You just want to show off. You're nothing. They'll eat you alive.

The men had four to six inches on her in height. No telling in weight. What would be gained in a competition?

Fun. Someone to play with. Someone with some skill. Sorry, Ron.

Walker bounced the ball to Larl. "You guys want to play? Two on two?"

Bobby looked over her head. "Where's the fourth player?" He gazed at her. "Oh, you mean you? Nah, that's no game."

Virgil smiled. "We could do it. We'll play half-court."

Walker shook her head. "Full court. NCAA rules." She motioned to the court. "Not exactly marked, but I think we know where the lines are."

Bobby laughed. "No way. You're a girl. You can't compete."

Walker smiled, her lips straight. "I can try."

Virgil studied her a moment. "You sure you want to do this?"

Walker nodded. "I don't get a lot of competition. I coach middle-school kids on the weekends. I'd love to play against some real opponents."

Virgil ducked his head. "Okay, I'm on your team."

Bobby and Larl exchanged opinions which Walker ignored. She walked to the middle of the court. "I'll throw it up." She grinned. "I'm too short to play center."

Bobby and Virgil faced off. Walker tossed the ball up, Bobby tapped it into play. Walker snagged it, drilled it to Virgil. They worked their way down the court, passing it back and forth, protecting it from the other two players. Walker fed Virgil the ball. He laid it in for the two points before Larl could reach him.

Walker met him under the basket for a high-five. "Nice job."

"Good passing."

Bobby sneered. "Luck."

Virgil chuckled. "Ignore him. He hates getting beat. Let's do it again."

The teams went back at it.

The score see-sawed. Walker and Virgil pulled ahead, then Bobby and Larl pulled even. Play remained clean until half an hour into the contest. Walker guarded Bobby from behind, refusing to let him advance up the court. Larl called, "Pass the ball, man!"

Bobby picked up his dribble. He held the ball chest high, then swung his elbow hard behind him. The move caught Walker directly in the eye, knocking her to the ground. She bounced to her feet, knocked the ball from his hands, and raced down the court to lay the ball in the basket.

Virgil and Larl screamed at Bobby. "Foul! Ejected! You can't do that!"

Bobby feigned surprise. "Was she behind me? I didn't see her."

Walker rejoined the three men. Blood dripped from her cheek. Her eye began swelling shut. She tossed the ball to Virgil. "Get ready."

"No. We're done. That's not how we play the game." He swung on Bobby. "You pull that stunt in a game, you get ejected. The team loses. Coach would bench your anatomy for the season."

Bobby held his hands out wide. "What? I didn't do anything. I was checking around…"

Larl cut him off. "Forget it, man. I'm not playing with you, either. We play clean, or we don't play." He stepped into Bobby's face and glared him down.

Bobby chortled. "I get it. She's a girl, so I can't hit her, right?" He sidestepped Larl to leer at Walker.

Virgil snarled, "No, she's a player, so you can't hit her or anyone else. You were deliberate and calculated." He chested up his teammate. A fight would be imminent…

Walker stepped in to speak, but Virgil stopped her. "No. There's no excuse for it. If Coach were here, he'd be kicked off the team." He glared at Bobby, then smiled without mirth. "I'm going to be sure you are. I don't care whether you hit a guy, or a girl, or a goat. That's not what our team is about." He handed Walker his shirt. "Go wash your eye out with this. Get some ice."

Walker handed him back his shirt. "I've got towels in the tent. I'm fine. He didn't hurt me." Blood continued to drip from the cut above her brow. Her vision blurred, impeded by the swelling that threatened to close her eye completely.

Bobby laughed. "No? Let's play some more." He dribbled the ball, then bounced it hard at Walker. She caught it and stepped back on the court.

Virgil grabbed Bobby's arm. "You're done, I'm telling you. Let's go. Unless you want to walk back to town by yourself." He jerked Bobby away, then dipped his head to Walker. "I'm sorry. I am. I enjoyed teaming with you."

Walker nodded. "I enjoyed the competition and the workout.

Maybe I can come watch your team if you play while we're still here."

"I'll check the schedule." He looked at Bobby, ordering, "Get in the *car*, man." He shoved Bobby toward the rise.

Bobby caught his balance and walked up the hill. Larl waved a hand at Walker. "Good game. Sorry he's a jerk." He started to add something, but Virgil yelled, "Let's go, Larl." He waved again and raced up the slope.

Walker watched the men disappear over the hill. She went to the tent, grabbed a hand towel, grabbed ice from the freezer, placed it over her eye. She sat on the table and sighed. She smiled. "Thanks, Lord. That's the most fun I've had…in a long time."

Can you say it?

Since he died? No. Nothing's been fun since him. Nothing will ever match that time. Nothing.

She dabbed at her eye. What would she tell Ron? She practiced some lines. "I got attacked by a rabid groundhog." No. Groundhogs don't get rabies. "Aliens." Might work. If aliens played roundball. "Slammed my ball into the ground. It bounced up and hit me." That one could work if he didn't examine it too close. He might buy it. Maybe. Or maybe she should stick with the aliens.

Walker pulled out her ball cap, put it on, tugged it low on her forehead. Maybe he wouldn't notice. Maybe no one would.

Fat chance.

How about the truth? You were you. Showing off. Being stupid. Thinking you can play with the big boys. Thinking you can play, period.

Ron knows the truth about you. Everyone knows the truth about you. You have no right to be around good people like these. Even the guys who were here are better than you.

You are loved. You are forgiven. You are accepted.

Walker sagged. "Who am I, Lord? When will I be enough?"

She walked to the tent and stretched out on her bed. She closed her eyes. No tears. They were as forbidden as showing pain. No tears. No release. Only silence.

~

The team returned after dark. Walker avoided Ron long enough for the men and women to split into their halves of the tent without him seeing her eye.

Maria caught her before lights out. "What did you do?" She moved back and forth to inspect Walker's injury from different angles.

Walker eyed her sideways. "Would you believe aliens?"

"No."

"Didn't think so." Walker and Maria sat on Walker's cot. Two other women sat across from them to listen to the explanation. "Bobby—you remember Bobby?—and two friends showed up after you were gone. We started a friendly game of hoops that turned ugly. Bobby elbowed me in the eye. The other two hauled him off after apologizing."

Maria shook her head, then lifted her eyes to Heaven. "Lord, thank You for taking care of Walker. She could have been seriously hurt or worse. Give us wisdom on how to go forward with this mission. I have a bad feeling about things. I don't like it. Show us what You want from us."

Walker hung her head. She added her prayers to Maria's. "Lord, I should have been grateful for Your protection. I didn't see it at the time. Help me see You. Help me know You."

You'll never know Him. He doesn't want to know you. You're trash.

Walker breathed out slowly. "Jesus, show me."

Maria ended. "Amen." She looked across the tent towards the men's side. "Ron is not going to be happy about this."

Walker nodded. "Okay, so playing ball wasn't smart. I admit it. But what should I have done?"

Maria stared at the canvas floor. "I don't know. Maybe gone to Pastor Mars' office to stay with him." She shrugged. "But that still would leave you unsupervised with a man." She sighed. "I suspect Ron will say you have to go with us tomorrow wherever we end up. He might not let you work, but at least you'll be safe."

"I still need to inspect those houses on the north side, plus the last one on the cul-de-sac."

Keisha, a second-year science major, joined the conversation. Her face darkened, her eyes grew serious. "I heard five people died in the house."

Walker's head snapped up sharply. "What?" She leaned forward to be closer. Her insides went still. She focused on every word.

"Yeah, the homeowner we were working with told us. There was a family of four. They were killed in the storm." Keisha shook her head, scowling.

Maria held up a hand. "You said five." Walker watched the woman sitting cross-legged on her bed, pulling at the covers. Maria's fingers worked over the silky trim on the blankets. Walker knew it was her friend's way of drawing serenity from the texture. *We all have our quirks, don't we?*

Some quirkier than others.

Keisha continued with her story. "There was a fifth person there. They think maybe a family friend or visitor. There wasn't any identification on the man, but someone in the neighborhood said the family probably knew him." Keisha rubbed the cuticle on her thumb as she spoke. Both thumbs were raw. She'd been fine when they left Oakton. Poor woman.

Walker had to ask, "Did they find his body in the same location as the rest of the family?" Her shoulders tightened. Her body went on heightened alert. Wrong. The story was all wrong.

Keisha shrugged. "I don't know that part. The homeowner just said what they'd heard." She sat back to lean on her hands.

Maria turned to Walker. "What are you thinking?" She lay the blanket down with deliberate motions. Must have caught herself.

Walker shook her head. "Nothing. Except I need to go check it out. First thing in the morning, if Ron agrees."

"You'll have to ask him. Once he sees your eye, I don't know how he'll feel about you going off from the group. Even with a chaperone." Maria held her hands out, palms up.

Keisha laughed. "Yeah, disaster seems to follow you around." The freshman rolled off Walker's cot and found her own. She climbed in, pulling the covers up.

Walker relaxed her shoulders. "Well, we'll have to see in the morning. Let's get the lights out before"—she added louder—"Ron yells at us."

Maria chuckled. She lifted her voice as well. "Housemother. That's him."

A voice called from across the partition. "I heard that."

Maria called back, "No, you didn't. Good night, boys."

Lights went out. Walker lay on her cot and stared at the top of the tent. Lessons of warnings from the past floated through her head. *"Hired arsonists tend to die in the fire they're paid to set. Dead men tell no tales."* Was the "family friend" the arsonist? What made the house at the cul-de-sac different? It was the only house where there had been fatalities. Even as backwater as Rallins might be, they still had early warning sirens. No one should have been caught unawares.

Something wasn't right. Walker knew it in her gut. She needed to see the house. Tomorrow. Early. She closed her eyes, then opened them again. She sighed, slid out of her cot, and hit her knees. She whispered, "Lord, You used me to save Alissa. Maybe You're using me to reveal Bobby for who he is. If my purpose in being here is to expose a killer, show me what to do. My life doesn't mean anything. All that matters is Your will and the people I can help. Use me. In Jesus' Name, amen."

Walker climbed back into her cot, closed her eyes. She whispered, "Don't let anyone else get hurt, please." She emptied her mind and slept.

MONDAY

Morning proved Maria correct. Ron insisted Walker accompany the crew to the new worksite. But she had been given strict orders to sit and watch. No mouth, no pouting, just sit. He did allow her to carry water bottles to the group, but nothing more strenuous. The whole group would walk to the house in the cul-de-sac so she could examine it before they left the area. Promise.

Walker sat on the grass slope nearest the workers, under an elm tree the tornado missed in its passage. Puffy clouds in the deep blue sky sailed slowly between the leaves. Walker knew people saw shapes in the swirls. She'd never had the privilege of sitting to imagine animals or objects as they floated by. She peered hard, trying to catch a vision of something, anything, as they passed.

Ron walked over. "What are you staring at? You look like you're searching for UFOs."

"I'm trying to see the shapes."

"Don't try so hard. Let your imagination…oh, right. You weren't allowed imagination, were you?"

Walker shrugged. "We managed a little when we weren't under strict surveillance."

Ron sat beside her on the bank. "I heard you share your testimony one Sunday night. I can't imagine growing up the way you did." He plucked a piece of grass and stuck it in his mouth.

Walker smiled without mirth. "Be glad." She mirrored his

action. She immediately spit it out. Yuk. What did that prove?

"And grateful." Ron stared at the sky.

"True." Walker stared where Ron pointed. A cumulus cloud puffed into a giant snowball. What else could she see? Marshmallows. Cotton balls. Nothing living.

Jun passed by. "Is this an official break? Can I join?" The math major dusted his gloves off on his jeans.

Ron waved to the front yard. "Pick a patch of grass and sit. We're talking about our upbringings."

Jun sat but shook his head. "I will pass on those memories." He lay back on the slight rise to stare at the sky.

Walker reached out to tap his knuckles. He returned the gesture. Ron leaned back on his elbows. "Okay, I agree. But you know God can—"

Jun and Walker both intoned, "—redeem even your worst days." Walker continued. "We know, Ron. I believe He can. I haven't seen Him do it yet. That's all." She sat back to let the damp grass have her frustrations. Maybe it would find a good use for them.

Ron raised his eyebrows. "No? How about you being able to see the arson at the church? Which none of the rest of us have the background to do? I'd say that's redemption." He kept his eyes on Walker, waiting for her response.

Walker stared at the ground. She came back with a question. "Do you think Pastor Mars thinks the same thing?"

Ron sat forward. "Why do you say that?" He stared at Walker intently.

Walker plucked at the grass, refusing to look up. "I saw his eyes when I told him about it. He wasn't happy I found it." The twitch. The reddening of the cheeks. The stammer.

"Maybe because it would slow up the rebuilding?" Ron raised an eyebrow.

"There was more." Walker tossed the blade of grass she held and plucked another. "He seemed embarrassed, like a kid caught with his hand in the cookie jar." She lifted her gaze to meet Ron's eyes. "I think he torched it himself. I think he saw the damage and thought, 'Why not?' No one would bother to check, really. It would all be storm damage. His congregation would get the new church they needed."

Ron stayed silent. Jun shook his head. "Why do you think that? He's a good man. Brother Matt talks highly of him." He sat up to stare at Walker.

Walker ducked her head to the side. "Whoever set the fire didn't know how to hide what they were doing. They did an amateur job. It wasn't done by someone professional or someone with experience. Beginner arson. I think Pastor Mars saw an opportunity and took it." She tossed the blade of grass. "Not that I blame him. The church needed to be demolished and rebuilt from the ground up. I hope the insurance thinks the same."

Ron's eyes narrowed. "Are you going to tell the arson investigator what you suspect?"

"Not unless he asks. My assignment is to search for signs of arson and flag them. That's what I'm doing. No one asked me to investigate or give my opinions." Walker gazed off down the street.

"If you're asked?" Ron pressed the issue.

Walker snorted. "I won't be. I'm a kid, right? Not a professional. They'll make their own determinations."

Jun's jaw dropped. "You would let Pastor Mars get away without consequence for his action?" His eyes widened in shock.

Walker glanced at the sky. "He didn't order the tornado. He didn't set it in motion or determine its path. He saw a chance to better his people's lives and took it. I think the rest is between him and God." She held Jun's gaze and waited.

Ron continued to eye Walker, his eyes filled with pity. "You give grace to others, but never yourself. Why?" He shook his head.

Walker lowered her eyes. "I have to live by a higher standard."

"Higher than God's?"

Walker turned on him. Bitterness filled her voice. "No. Not higher than His. But I don't know what His standards are for me. I know what my background said. I know what got drilled into me. It's what is, Ron. It's what I know."

Before the conversation could continue, a silver sedan pulled over in front of them. Walker and company stopped talking to see who the driver might be. What they might want.

A middle-aged man, well-dressed and coiffed, slid out of the driver's seat. An equally smart-looking woman remained in the shotgun position. The man smiled as he approached. "Morning, people."

Ron nodded his head. "Good morning." Ron, Walker, and Jun rose to their feet.

"You're the relief team from Oakton, am I correct? Pastor Mars said I would find you here." The man stood on the sidewalk in front of them. Walker eyed him.

Ron nodded. "We're some of the team." He pointed to the semi-demolished house across the street. "The rest of them are working over there."

The man didn't turn. He continued to smile. "Are you the leader of this group? Ron Jennings?"

Ron stood. "I am. You are?"

"Greg Willis." He extended his hand. Ron wiped the dirt from his palm, then shook Willis' hand. Mr. Willis said, "I'm the County Controller. Also, the assistant coach at our community college, and part of the school board." He drew a card from his pocket and handed it to Ron. While Ron examined it, the man continued, "I hear you have a basketball expert on your team." Walker noticed Willis did not bother with either Jun or her. *He's making his case for something. Knows he has to go through channels.*

Keep a close eye on him.

Always.

Willis shifted from one foot to another. "Our kids are back in school to get some normalcy back in their lives. But our high school woman's Phys Ed teacher is still out with a broken leg. The high school principal asked if I knew anyone who could supervise the girls' classes. They're in the basketball rotation. When I heard you had an expert, I thought we might be able to entice her away for a few hours a day. It's only for a week. Can you spare her?" He glanced over at the work crew as if searching for the likely suspect.

Ron stared at the ground a moment. He chewed on his lips, then turned to Walker. "What do you think? Can you handle a P.E. class?"

Walker directed her questions to Willis. "How many students in each class?"

"Usually twenty." Willis shifted his attention to Walker.

"How many classes each day?" *Will it leave me time to inspect houses?*

"Five each day." He smiled at her. *Watch the eyes. Something is hidden there. I don't know what, but there is something in the back of them.*

"What grades?" *How many smart-mouth teens will challenge me about my age?*

"Eight through twelve." Willis eyed Walker, his head tilted. "Are you the expert?"

Walker began to speak, but Ron interrupted her. "Yes, she's the one you've heard about. She's the basketball wiz. Mr. Willis, this is Walker." Ron started to put his hand on her shoulder, but pulled it back. He added, "She volunteers at the community centers, so she has a clean background check. We all had to be cleared to come on this trip, in case we worked with families with children. We can have the paperwork emailed to you if you want."

Willis' eyes moved up and down over Walker's figure. He raised his eyebrows. "Well, what do you think, Ms. Walker?" He turned back to Ron. "Will you spare her for a few days?" *Not "can," "will." He's smooth. He bears watching. Carefully.*

Ron smiled. "As long as you give her back at the end of each day. I have to keep track of my flock." Ron grinned at Walker. "Can you keep from being injured?"

Walker sneered at him. "Yes." *Your body votes no.*

I didn't ask for a vote.

Ron turned serious. "Do you want to do this?"

Walker looked at Willis, then turned back to Ron. "Yes. At least there, I can be useful."

"Can you start today? Now?" Willis took a half-step forward.

Walker's eyes flared wide. Ron cleared his throat. "Um, I don't know how we can get her there. We'd have to pull the entire team. Even if you were prepared to take her, she can't...."

Willis smiled. "Ah, yes. Pastor Mars told me about your 'no males alone with females' policy. Which, I'll say, is a great one. Fortunately, my wife accompanied me here." He pointed to the car. "I had faith we would be able to recruit you." He nodded to Walker.

Ron faced her. "Your call if you want to go." His eyes were steady, waiting for her response.

Walker eyed Willis a moment. The internal voices were silent. She nodded. "Okay. I'll go now." She pointed to Ron. "Stay safe. Keep the team the same way."

Ron nodded. "Always. We'll hit the cul-de-sac home tonight after you get back."

Walker turned and followed Willis to the car. He opened the back door for her. She slid in. The woman in front turned to smile at Walker. Walker read honesty and sincerity in the woman's eyes. She extended her hand. "Hi. I'm Patricia Willis."

"Walker."

Mr. Willis slid behind the driver's seat. "Ms. Walker has volunteered to supervise the girls' classes."

Patricia gave Walker an authentic smile of appreciation. "Thank you very much. I know it will mean everything to our students. They need to get their lives back to normal as much as possible."

"I hope I can help." Walker settled back in the seat, ready to ride the remainder of the trip in silence.

Patricia asked, "Have you chosen your major yet?"

Walker leaned forward. "Yes, ma'am. I'm studying to be a

social worker. I'm in my second year."

The woman laughed. "My mistake. You seem a bit younger than a sophomore."

"I skipped some grades." *Tested out early, thanks to Brother Golding.*

"You must be quite knowledgeable."

Walker demurred. "Highly trained." She shut down the voices taunting her.

"Where did you go to school?" Mrs. Willis' questions seemed more than just polite chatter.

Walker gave Patricia her standard line. "I studied the last four years in Oakton, ma'am."

Greg interrupted his wife's interrogation, friendly as it might have been. "What happened to your eye, young woman?"

Walker registered his gaze in the rearview mirror as neutral. "A disgruntled basketball player objected to being covered tightly on the court. They expressed their dissatisfaction by throwing an elbow."

Patricia scowled. "I hope she got ejected."

Walker shrugged. "It was an informal competition."

Greg's eyes narrowed. "I've been made aware of the incident. Virgil informed me what happened."

Patricia turned to her husband. "What? Virgil? How would he know?"

"He was there." Greg gazed in the mirror. "I'm an assistant coach with the men's team. Bobby has been cut permanently."

Walker shook her head. "Not on my account, please." *I don't need enemies. More enemies.*

"No. His elbowing you became his last straw, so to speak. He'd been on probation for misconduct in other games. I warned him getting himself ejected did our team no favors. One more exhibition of aggression in a game would get him thrown off. Virgil and Larl said you gave him no provocation for his response." Greg's eyes smiled. "Your discretion is appreciated, though. You could have reported the matter, and all three boys would have been in trouble."

Patricia turned over the back of the seat. "I want to know how you ended up in a game with three men you hardly know?" She smiled, but her voice held an undertone of concern.

Walker lowered her eyes. "The team left me alone to rest yesterday. Bobby, Virgil, and Larl showed up after the others left. I'd been stretching by working out. We talked basketball and started a friendly game."

Patricia stared hard at Walker. "I've seen you before. You…" She stopped. A light of recognition filled her eyes. "You were the one who rescued Alissa."

"I found them. I didn't rescue them."

"Alissa says you kept them alive when the dresser fell. That counts as rescuing them in my book." Patricia's eyes narrowed. "You were signing on the news broadcast. Why?"

No tells. Stay smooth. "I develop a debilitating stutter when I'm in a crowd. It's easier to sign than to talk."

Patricia lifted her head. "Ah, I see. Very wise."

Greg half-smiled. "Yes, it is. I should learn how to do it for my speeches."

Patricia grinned. "Yes, you should, dear. It might make your speeches far more intelligible."

He sneered in good-natured humor. "Thank you for your support."

Patricia didn't ask more questions. Walker moved the conversation along. "What work are you engaged in, Mrs. Willis?"

"I'm a trophy wife." Greg groaned. Patricia smiled. "Our children are grown and gone, so my primary occupation is housewife or home keeper or 'industrial engineer' as I think the new title is." She laughed. "I recently went back to school to pursue my bachelor's in financial management." She smiled again. "So, I can keep up with the millions my husband makes, according to the neighbors."

In the rearview mirror, Walker watched Greg roll his eyes.

Walker chuckled. "I understand how neighbors are. Always suspicious you have a bit more than they do."

Greg grumbled. "About right."

Walker turned the questioning. "You said you were an assistant coach. Is it your full-time position?"

"I'm the county controller during the day. My sports alter-ego only comes out at night."

"I see. You both have multi-faceted lives."

Patricia chuckled. "Which is a polite way of saying we have split personalities. Thank you."

Walker lowered her eyes but smiled.

Another fifteen minutes brought the car to a red-brick, multi-storied building. Greg pulled around the front half-circle drive-thru. "I'll let you two out here and park the car. Patricia, if you would introduce Ms. Walker to Principal Douglas?" *He questions, not orders. Nice.*

There's an ulterior motive. Men never ask. They order.

"Men, love your wives." They are capable.

Not in our experience.

Walker followed Patricia through the entryway to a glass-enclosed office. A uniformed security officer sat at a gunmetal gray desk. The walls were industrial-yellow cinderblocks painted with the school's logo and mascot. Clipboards hung on both sides of the entrance. A phone sat on a desktop cluttered with files and papers. The man rose as the two women entered. He smiled at Patricia. "Mrs. Willis! Nice to see you here." He extended his hand.

Patricia returned the handshake. "Leon, this is Ms. Walker." She tilted her head. "I don't know your first name, dear."

"It's just Walker, ma'am. People call me Walker."

Her eyes flared, but only slightly. "Ms. Walker, then. She will be substituting for Marjory Hinton until she can be on her feet again. Ms. Walker is with the relief team from Oakton."

Leon held out his hand to Walker. "Ms. Walker. Welcome."

No gun. Low perception of threat level.

Bobby should make them rethink that.

Doubtful.

Patricia continued talking. "Greg asked me to take her to meet Principal Douglas."

Leon handed Patricia one of his clipboards. "She's down in the gym right now. If you will both sign in, please."

"I'll take Ms. Walker there. She can get the feel of her new office." Patricia smiled, then filled out the lines and handed the board back to the security officer.

Leon pushed a buzzer under his desk. The main entrance swung open. Walker ducked her head. "Thank you." She walked with Mrs. Willis down a hall lined with lockers and open classroom doors.

As they turned the first corner, Patricia asked, "Why no first name?"

Walker debated. "I haven't chosen one yet."

Patricia nodded. "I see." Her eyes sparkled. "I'm partial to Patricia."

"It's a beautiful name."

"What are you thinking of?"

Walker took several steps before answering. "Something less identifying, gender-wise. People won't see the name and automatically form an opinion based on their preference."

Patricia nodded. "Smart." She pointed to the double doors at the end of the hall. "Down here."

Before they reached the gym, Greg rejoined them. "Ladies."

Walker stopped and looked around. She missed something. It took a moment, but she asked, "Why is it so quiet? Where's the hubbub? I haven't seen a single student in the halls."

Greg pursed his lips. "Good eye. And ear. We're still down in attendance. Some of our students are staying with relatives across the county, so they can't return to classes yet. I think we're still only at a little less than half our enrollment."

"But you're starting anyhow?"

Greg nodded. "We have to begin sometime. We'll work out a

make-up program down the road with the ones who missed resumption of classes."

"I see." *Not sure I agree, but you didn't ask my opinion.*

No, he did not. Keep it to yourself.

The three entered the gym. Typical gymnasium configuration. Roof to rafters to the third floor. Hardwood pine floors. Shiny, well administrated. The squeak of athletic wear. The smells of sweat and industrial cleaners. A woman in a dark skirt-suit, black nylons, and no shoes paced the sidelines. She shouted encouragement or instruction as needed at the ten players on the court. Mostly instruction. Maybe in her fifties. Gray hair pulled tightly back in a bun. Walker turned her attention to the players, assessing their skill, or lack thereof. Definitely lack. She shook her head.

Greg noticed. "They have heart. Not much else. Marjory lettered in volleyball."

"I see." *I do. No future in basketball for women. Volleyball, maybe. Not hoops.* The insults of childhood mocked her. Walker tamped them down. She walked with her benefactors to meet Ms. Douglas.

The woman glared as the Willis's approached. She called out, "Why did you bring me another student? You promised me an instructor." She scowled.

Greg made the introductions. "Ms. Douglas, this is Ms. Walker. She *is* your substitute instructor." He motioned for Walker.

Walker stepped forward, extended her hand. "Ms. Douglas."

The principal stared Walker up and down. "You're a teacher? Where?"

Patricia offered, "She coaches in Oakton. She has volunteered to step in for a week or so until Marjory returns."

Walker didn't bother to correct the wording. The job here, now, was to impress this woman. Show her Walker could handle the task in front of them.

Douglas asked, "What do you know about basketball?"

"Everything."

Douglas raised her eyebrows. "Cocky much?" She folded her arms over her chest.

"No, ma'am. Not at all. I love the game. I have spent my time researching all I can about the sport. Peach baskets to now." Walker held her eyes. *Ask me anything. Anything at all. Steady. No wiggling. No movement. Stand still. Stand strong.*

"Are you any good at it?" The woman stepped into a wider stance. Challenging.

Greg interjected, "According to Virgil and your son, she's very good at it." He chuckled. "They wanted to recruit her for our team."

Larl is your son?

Ms. Douglas' eyes flared, then hardened. "I apologize for my son being where he shouldn't have been. He knew better." A woman who takes no guff.

Walker defended the young men. "They couldn't know my team had already left for a worksite." Would the woman hold the game against her?

"They should have left immediately." She studied Walker's eye. "Bobby do that to you?"

"Yes, ma'am." No sense denying what she already knew.

"No loss to the team. They'll do better without him." She nodded to Greg and Patricia. "Thank you. I'll take her over from here."

Patricia stage-whispered behind her hand, "She really does have a cuddly side. She has to hide it from the students, but she's a teddy bear inside."

Ms. Douglas' eyes sparkled, but her face remained in its scowl. "Do not talk to me about cuddly. I'll have you running laps again."

Patricia threw up her hands in mock alarm. "No, ma'am! No, ma'am."

Ms. Douglas blew her whistle. Greg took Patricia's elbow and led his wife away. He called, "We'll see you get back to your encampment tonight."

Walker waved, then turned back to watch the girls on the court assemble around Ms. Douglas. The older woman motioned to Walker. "This is Ms. Walker. She'll be subbing for a week. You will treat her with the same respect you treat me. Does everyone understand?"

Heads nodded. Walker saw some eyes cast at her, away, and back again.

Sizing up the sub.

Do not show fear.

Walker smiled back at the class. "Good morning, ladies."

Ms. Douglas handed Walker the whistle. She pointed to a clipboard on a bench. "Class roster. I've already taken attendance for this group. Make sure the attendance sheets get turned in at the end of the day."

She looked back at the class. "Anyone caught cutting class will be spending afternoons in my office. Understood?"

Ten voices echoed, "Yes, Ms. Douglas."

The woman picked up her shoes, then exited the gym. Walker eyed the class. "Names, please."

She watched the eyes closely. Three in, she detected the fake. Four and five wore smirks. So did nine and ten. Walker swallowed her reaction, walked to the clipboard, picked it up. "Says here we have May, Taylor, Bee, and Lisa in class." She indicated the four imposters. "Step forward, please."

The girls exchanged glances, stepped forward. Walker held them in an even gaze. "Giving the sub a hard time is universal. I know the game." She pointed to the six girls who had answered truthfully. Walker repeated each name. In order. Without checking the clipboard. She raised an eyebrow. "May. Taylor. Bee. Lisa." Three sets of eyes twitched. One widened, then narrowed. Walker stepped in front of the first girl. "May." She stepped again. "Taylor." "Bee." Lisa." The last two girls were twins. Identical enough to be confusing for some teachers. Walker smiled at the four girls. "Back in line."

Only May tried to keep up the ruse. "My name is Carly

Witherspoon."

Walker shrugged. "If that's the lie you want to die on, fine." She lay the whistle with the clipboard. "This is a mandatory rotation. Who loves the game?"

Six hands went in the air. "Who is on the intramural team?"

Taylor cleared her throat. "We don't have one."

"Why not?" *Because they're girls. Girls can't play ball. Girls can't play anything. They only pretend.*

The girls stared at each other. "They don't offer one."

"Do you want one?" Most of the girls nodded. "Have you petitioned to have a team?"

"Carly" laughed. Harshly. "We did. Girls' sports don't make the money boys' sports do. In case you didn't notice, we're sort of a depressed area, you know? Not a lot of money to go around. The last tax levy was voted down, so the school had to make cuts. Girl's teams were the first thing they cut. That was four years ago, and they've never been offered since."

Walker raised her eyebrows. "Do you want to play?" This would be the leader.

Carly stabbed her hand to her hip. "Yeah, but…"

Walker cut her off. "Do you want to play?" She spaced each word carefully.

The girl glanced at her classmates, then back at Walker. "Yeah."

"Let's give the people something to watch they'll pay for." She pointed to the balls against the wall. "Everyone take one." The girls complied. "I want to see you dribble."

Groans. "We all know how to dribble a ball." Carly's eyes rolled.

"Show me." The girls began bouncing the balls. "Run." Some held the balls in their hands to run. "No, I mean run while you're dribbling."

A few managed a start. Those who couldn't, Walker pointed to. "Pick it up. Walk. Dribble and walk. Then increase your speed."

Four of the girls dribbled slowly with deliberate motions. Bounce. Bounce. Bounce.

Those who could, she ordered, "Faster."

Carly stared hard. She dribbled the ball, standing still. "Which? Dribbling or running?"

"Yes. Do it. Show me how fast you can do both." Carly nodded to her crew. The six girls ran, dribbling the ball in time up and down the court.

Walker watched the more proficient girls for a few moments. "Switch hands." Hmmm. Less skilled with their non-dominant hand. Of course. "Back and forth between hands."

Balls sailed to the far side of the court. Girls raced to retrieve them, then started over. Carly kept a decent pace until Walker ordered, "Behind your back."

Carly fell out, finally. She glared at Walker. "You do it."

Walker stepped in front of the young woman. "How old are you?" Walker needed to bring this one into line. Win her, Walker would have the rest of the class without issue.

"Fifteen." Carly stared Walker down.

Walker shrugged. "Let's do this. We'll have a competition. You fall out before I do, you listen and do what you're told the rest of the week. I fall out, you teach the class. I won't tell Ms. Douglas."

Carly's eyes narrowed. She looked around at the class. Girls urged, "Do it. Go for it. Try it."

Carly nodded. "Sure." She lifted her head, daring Walker to back down.

Walker pointed to Taylor. "You call the switches. We'll both be surprised at the same time." She challenged the caller. "Make the cadence fast."

Taylor nodded. "Yes, ma'am." She waited until Walker and Carly had their balls at the ready. "Go. Dribble."

Carly began at an average pace. Walker doubled the girl's speed. Carly noted and picked hers up. Walker increased hers.

"Left hand."

Walker switched without losing a beat. Carly took a moment to adjust but continued without losing the ball.

"Run."

Walker and Carly raced up the sidelines. Carly tried to match Walker. Walker increased her speed again.

"Back and forth."

Walker's ball became a blur. Carly stayed with her but couldn't equal the speed.

"Behind the back."

Carly managed four passes side-to-side before she lost control of the ball. She stomped to the sidelines and flopped down on the bleacher seat. Walker slowed her dribbling but kept the ball moving. She held Carly's eyes. "Very nice. You've got definite skills. I can see you've been working at it." Walker let her talent fly. In, out, over, behind, under, through…across the court, out to the center line. She lifted the ball into a rainbow that sailed through the net.

Walker retrieved the ball. She walked back to stand in front of the girls. All eyes were on her. The only one who mattered now was Carly. She held the fifteen-year-old's glare. "Learn. That's why you're here. I'm here to teach you. Do you want to learn?"

Carly stared back. And back. And back. "Yeah, I want to learn." She nodded. Case won.

"Good. It'll make the week easier for both of us." Walker bounced the ball to Carly. "Show me free throws." She held the class in her eyes. "Free throws are free points. Games can come down to that difference. There is no reason to miss them. None. You're standing alone at a line, no one coming at you, no one trying to block your shot. You should never, ever, ever miss a free throw."

One of the girls offered, "Yeah, but players do it all the time." She threw the ball up and missed.

"Not an excuse." Walker smiled. "I'll give a pass from running to the first person who can tell me who holds the single-game record for most free throws."

Guesses were thrown out. "Jordan." "Curry." "Harden."

"Davis."

"Nope. Adrian Dantley. Back in 1983. He hit twenty-eight in one game." Walker looked around. "Twenty-eight free points his opponents had to make up. Who had the longest streak for free throws?"

She continued her history lessons as the girls practiced their shots. The bell rang. Walker dismissed the class. "Carly."

The girl turned. "Ma'am?"

"You've got skills. You can be the leader here. Do it." Walker chuckled. "Why'd you pick Carly?"

The girl stared at the ground. "Because I hate the name May. I get made fun of all the time. 'May I this' or 'May I that.' And those are the innocent ones." Her eyes burned. "Guys are far more expressive."

"Fair enough. When you're eighteen, you can change your name to anything you want. It won't change who you are. That, you're stuck with. So, make it good, whatever you're called."

Carly stared at Walker for several moments, then nodded once and left for the showers. Walker shook her head. "Carly. Yeah, it rings better than May." She picked up the clipboard, readying herself for the next class.

~

The periods went by. Girls were older, girls were younger. Some were gifted. Some weren't. Sharing the knowledge of a passion Walker held made the day fly. Sixth period ended. The bell rang the students home. Walker put the balls away. She couldn't resist a few last shots. Free throw line. Top of the key. NCAA three-point line. NBA three-point line. Half-court. Step back from half-court. She missed the last one.

"Hey, she's human! She missed a shot."

Walker turned to see Carly and her friends hanging at the door to the gym. "Go home, ladies. I'll see you tomorrow."

The girls walked to sit on the benches. Book bags and books

piled on the floor. Carly eyed Walker closely. "Where are you from? Where did they find you?"

Walker smiled. "Under a rock. Where else?" Carly scowled at her. Walker chuckled. "I'm with the relief team that came from Oakton. I'm a sophomore in college." She nodded. "Yes, I'm only a year or two older than you are. I'm eighteen."

Taylor asked, "Why are you here? Here, here. Teaching, I mean."

"Mr. Willis heard I taught roundball. He thought I could fill in for a week or so. I agreed, so here I am." The girls muttered between themselves.

Carly nudged the floor. "Would you consider staying longer?" She looked up, hope in her eyes.

Walker shook her head. "I can't. I've got classes to finish in Oakton." She smiled. "You don't need me. You need to repeat what I've taught you. Over and over and over. It's how I learned. How I got to the level I am. Repetition. It's not magic. It's doing it over and over until it's muscle memory."

"Yeah, but our teacher doesn't even like basketball." Taylor didn't disguise the bitterness in her voice.

Walker raised her eyebrows. "You can change that. Talk to Ms. Douglas. She has a son who plays. She knows what passion is. Maybe she can get something restarted." Walker turned from girl to girl. "If she can't, there are always rec centers willing to try new things. If you go in with the willingness to serve, they will be happy to accommodate you. Trust me."

More girls drifted in from the hall. Walker gazed around the room. "Don't you have to go home? Or have homes to go to?"

Several shrugged. One girl offered, "Not really. No one's there. Mom doesn't mind if I hang around at school. The gym stays open until six, anyhow. Mostly to let the guys practice. But we can stay down at this end to work."

Walker rolled her eyes. "Fine." She shoveled the balls out of the bag. "Here. Shoot. Practice. Have fun." She picked up her clipboard. "I've got to turn this in. No one get hurt while I'm gone."

She left the girls and walked the attendance record to the principal's office. Ms. Douglas sat at her desk, flipping pages of paper. Walker tapped on the door. "May I come in?"

"Since you asked, yes." The woman held out her hand for the registers. "How did classes go?" She continued flipping the papers without looking up.

Walker smiled. "They went well, ma'am."

"Drop the ma'am." Ms. Douglas took the attendance sheets.

"They went well, Ms. Douglas. You have some talented basketball players. It's a shame there's nowhere for them to compete."

Ms. Douglas snorted. "Shame about a lot of things in this life." She stared at Walker. "What is it they want?"

Walker met the woman's eyes. "The chance to perform like the boys do. To get the same recognition for their efforts." Walker held Ms. Douglas' gaze.

"Don't want much, do they?" The corners of her mouth twitched. But not so as anyone else would notice. All they would see was the stern, disapproving glare of the school principal.

Walker saw enough to know. She presented her case. "Not to start, no. They want to compete." She pressed her advantage. "Like your son does. I saw his passion when we were on the court together. He loves the game. He's good at it. You've got some girls here equally talented. They want the chance to show it."

Ms. Douglas eyed Walker. Walker held her gaze. The older woman nodded. "I tell you what, Ms. Walker. I'll let you assemble two teams. I'll consider it if they can hold their own in a real game. And look like actual players."

Walker smiled. "Thank you, Ms. Douglas. I know the girls will appreciate it, too."

"They can show me by getting to class and staying in school." The woman's eyes were firm, challenging. She turned back to her papers.

Walker backed out of the door and returned to the gym. She called the girls around to let them know what the principal said. "Two teams. Competing against each other. You have to play like a team. Work like a team. You have to make it count." She gazed around the circle. "Who do you know who will be willing to learn, wants to play, and will stick with it?"

A few names were suggested. Walker nodded. "Call them. Get them here. I know it's only four-thirty, but we'll call it for tonight. Plan on staying after school tomorrow and the rest of the week. We've got a lot of work to do."

The girls disbanded and left. All except Carly. She eyed Walker sideways. "Why are you doing this? Why do you care about whether we have a team or not?"

"Because I know you." Walker sat on the bench. "I've been you." She sniffed. "I'm still you. You want something so bad it hurts. You'll do anything to be able to get it. Maybe I can make it easier for you than I had it. Maybe I can't, but I can try."

"Why, though? I mean, what, you just go around rescuing kids for no reason? It doesn't make sense."

Walker studied the floor. "It does when you know Some One Who did the same for you. Went to bat for you. Made a way so you could have something you've always wanted." She looked up. "But it wasn't basketball. It was life. I never knew what living was about. I knew hate. I knew anger. I knew wanting revenge. But life? Real life? I didn't know it. Didn't want to know it. Until I met a Man Who didn't want anything from me. Didn't want to use me or sell me or hurt me. Loved me and wanted to share His kind of life with me."

Her voice caught. "Took me a long time to believe it. Longer to accept it. But He was patient. He didn't let me go. I finally realized I couldn't live without Him. So now I owe Him my life with everything in me." She smiled at Carly. "Long answer is He did it for me, so I need to do it for others. Put myself out there. Help where I can. Be His hands and feet."

"So, you're a Jesus freak."

"I'm a Christ follower." Walker's voice caught again. "I owe Him, Carly. Literally owe Him my life. I'd be dead if it weren't for Him. Nothing He will ever ask of me is greater than He did for me. If it makes me a Jesus freak, I'll take the name and be proud of it."

Carly continued to study Walker. "How? How did he save you?"

Walker shook her head. "I'm not ready to share that. Not here and now." She smiled. "Let's do this in a less busy place, okay?" Walker's eyes lost focus on the now. She closed them. "It's not a story I'm proud of." She swallowed. "But He saved me. That's what counts."

Walker smiled. "Go home, Carly. I'll see you tomorrow."

Carly picked up her books, gave Walker a last glance, and walked out of the gym. Walker sighed. She lowered her head. "Lead me, Lord. If she is truly interested, I'll tell her the truth. But if she only wants to have something to tell others, I'm not ready to share my past. You know why. Show me what to do and when."

Walker walked the empty halls back to the principal's office. She checked in on Ms. Douglas. The older woman had gathered her canvas bag, the one with "Teacher's Rock" printed on the side, grabbed an armload of notebooks, and exited her office. She closed the door behind her. "Ms. Walker, Greg Willis called me a few minutes ago. He has been delayed at the office. He asked if I would take you to my home. He and Patricia will pick you up after he finishes at five."

Walker shook her head. "I don't want to be a lot of trouble. I can call my group. They can pick me up here. It would be less hassle for you."

Ms. Douglas sniffed. "Young woman, you were hired on the word of Greg Willis. While I trust his judgment, I would like to know more about the person supervising my students." Her eyes twinkled. "Especially one who is inciting them to form a team competition."

Walker drew in a deep breath. She let it out slowly. "Thank you for the invitation, ma'am. I will be honored to accompany you to your home."

Ms. Douglas eyed Walker sideways. "You can drop the charm, young woman."

Walker ducked her head. "I was taught to speak respectfully to my superiors."

"You do it well. I'm giving you permission to speak plainly."

The woman gave Walker "the eye." Walker smiled slightly. "I will. Thank you for taking me home."

"That's better. Let's go."

Walker followed Ms. Douglas to her car. The principal shoved her bag and the papers she carried into the back seat. The older woman cleared a stack of reports and notebooks off the cluttered front seat, so Walker had room to sit. When both women were in the car, Ms. Douglas admitted, "I don't often have riders."

Walker chuckled. "My roommate has the same issue with papers everywhere. She knows exactly where everything is, she tells me. I've never known her to lose something, but I can't figure out her system."

Ms. Douglas put the car in motion. "It does take time to learn it. Which is why I don't have passengers. Larl has offered to 'clean out my car,' but I told him if he touches it, I will rescind his right to bear children."

Walker could see the slightest reflection of a twinkle in the principal's eyes. She swallowed her own smile and nodded. "I understand."

They arrived at Ms. Douglas' home in under twenty minutes. The house stood on an acre of property which had been spared any wind damage. Stately oak and elm trees lined the front walk to the two-story brick house. The principal pulled the car around to the back to park. She and Walker exited the vehicle and entered the house. A warm country kitchen welcomed them. The walls were pale yellow trimmed in dark green. Floral café curtains covered the windows. A wood table sat in the center of the connected dining room, flanked by a rolling buffet cart and more chairs.

Ms. Douglas ordered, "Take a seat. I'm going to put my things away."

If "ma'am" wasn't allowed, "Ms. Douglas" would be almost as repetitive. Walker offered, "Thank you." The phrase would also get boring, but it worked for now. She chose a chair with her back nearest a wall. Away from any "sneak" approaches. Habit.

Ms. Douglas returned to the kitchen. "Drink? What kind? Soda, water, orange juice, coffee from this morning, iced tea…."

"Water, thank you." Watch the calories.

Yeah, you're getting pudgy around the middle.

Everywhere else, too. You need to exercise harder.

Run harder. Work harder. You never work hard enough.

Ms. Douglas gave her a glass of ice and water, poured one for herself, then sat at the table. "Now, the interrogation can begin." Her eyes twinkled. The corners of her mouth edged up.

Walker smiled. "What would you like to know?"

"Everything. Start at the beginning. Where were you born? Who are your parents? Siblings? Educational background. Elementary schools? Middle? High school? College? Boyfriends? I'm all ears." The woman smiled broadly, finally. "We can start with college. Where are you attending? What is your major?"

"I'm a sophomore at Ohio State University. *Go Bucs.* I'm studying to be a social worker."

"Why social work?"

"So, I can help kids get off the streets. Maybe keep some from going there to begin with."

Ms. Douglas' eyes pierced Walker's. "Personal experience?"

"Yes, ma'am." Walker lifted her head slightly.

The older woman ducked her head slightly. "I find those with the most passion for something have a direct connection to it. How long were you on the streets?"

Walker hesitated. "Technically, I'm still 'on the streets.' I live at a homeless shelter run by Brother Matt Golding. I've been there since I turned sixteen. He took me in, gave me a place to sleep and food to eat." Walker smiled at the floor. "All of us on the team have been with him at one point or another in our lives. That's why when he asked, we came."

"You're only eighteen now?"

"I skipped some grades."

"I see." Ms. Douglas tapped the table lightly. A subconscious habit. Not intended to mean pay attention. Walker noted the slight tap of the foot, the barely audible hum under the woman's breath. Not nervous. Movement for the sake of movement.

"So, you and your team come down here, you rescue a woman and her baby, get in a fight with one of our boys, then come to my school to teach. All in what, three days?"

Walker laughed. "Um, four, I think." She took a long swallow of her water.

"You've been busy."

The backdoor opened. Larl and Virgil entered. Larl hollered, "Hey, Mom!" before he came fully through the door. He stopped abruptly. "Oops. Didn't know you were there." He went over and kissed his mother's cheek. Virgil copied his friend's actions, kissing Ms. Douglas on the cheek as well. "Hey, Mom."

Mom?

Honorific. Not his biological mom. Listen.

Walker didn't react to the term. She smiled at the two young men. "Gentlemen."

Ms. Douglas snorted. "I wouldn't use that term for them. Heathens. Fit's closer."

Larl grinned. "Thanks, Mom. Way to make me look good in front of the new school marm." The young man began rummaging through the refrigerator. He grabbed a soda, tossed one to Virgil. The two males sat at the table with Ms. Douglas and Walker.

Ms. Douglas cocked her head at her son. "How do you know?"

"Coach Willis told us." He grinned at Walker. "After we told him about how you play roundball. So, you can thank us for your new gig."

Virgil laughed. "Also getting you away from swinging a sledgehammer."

Walker nodded. "I thank you."

Ms. Douglas continued her questioning. "You teach basketball?"

"I coach at the local rec centers. Little people up to high school. It's a way to give back."

"Plus stay connected to the sport, correct?" The principal drank from her glass.

"Yes." Walker shrugged. "I love the game. I'll do anything I can do that keeps me involved."

Ms. Douglas smiled. "So, you have two passions. Basketball and helping kids get off the streets. Anything else?"

Staying alive.

Staying out of jail.

I made recompense. I'm clear.

Sure, you are.

Walker smiled. "Right now, it's about as much as I have time for. Between volunteering and studying, there's not much left."

Ms. Douglas nodded. "I remember those days." She stretched slightly, then stared at her phone.

Must have it on vibrate.

"It's from Greg Willis. Seems he's been delayed longer than he expected. They won't be here until after six."

Walker leaned forward. "I really can call my team to get me. I don't want to disrupt your evening."

"You're not disrupting anything." Ms. Douglas stretched in her chair.

Larl suggested, "I can run her back to the church."

Walker shook her head. "I appreciate it, but I'm not permitted to ride with a man alone."

He peered at her sideways. "You're an adult, right? Over eighteen?"

"I'm eighteen, yes. But while I'm on this team, I represent Brother Matt's mission. He has strict rules about men and women not riding together with people who aren't their spouses. Scripture says to 'avoid any appearances of misconduct.' I won't violate his constraints."

Ms. Douglas smiled. "I will need to meet this Brother Matt one day. He sounds like an incredible person."

"He is."

Virgil asked, "So that means you can't date, either?"

"Only in groups. Or we meet in public places." She nodded. "I know, it sounds very old-fashioned. It's contrary to culture today. But it keeps us safe from whispers and trouble."

Ms. Douglas tapped the table with intent. "Hear, hear. We could use a little more 'old-fashioned' common sense."

Larl groaned. Virgil echoed him. Ms. Douglas held both young men in her stern gaze. "Wait until you have children. Especially daughters. You'll see things differently."

Larl quipped, "If I can't date, I won't have to worry about it, will I?"

Ms. Douglas raised both eyebrows and glared at her son. "Excuse me?"

Larl smiled. "Only joking, Mom. Only joking."

The principal stood. "Since the Willis's are going to be late, why don't I fix dinner for all of us?" She turned her eye on Virgil. "I assume you're staying for dinner?"

"I'd love to, thanks. Mom's out of town." Virgil slumped in his chair, draping his arm over the seat back.

"What is this, the third time this month? She should be hunting for a different job."

Virgil nodded. "That's what Dad tells her. But she likes what she does, and the money is good."

Larl asked, "What's for dinner?"

Ms. Douglas pulled a tray from the freezer. "Lasagna. I've got some I made last week and froze. It'll be ready in about forty-five minutes."

Walker pulled out her phone. "I honestly can call my people to come for me."

Ms. Douglas waved her off. "Tell them you'll be late and home after dinner. We pulled you out here. The least we can do is feed you a home-cooked meal."

The older woman glared at her, almost daring Walker to say no. Walker smiled. "I'll text my group leader. He'll appreciate knowing where I am."

Virgil's jaw dropped. "You have to check in, too? They really treat you like little kids."

Walker shook her head. "We treat each other like street kids. If someone goes missing, we assume the worst. Someone has been kidnapped, maybe hurt, maybe in the hospital, maybe fell off the wagon. We have to check out for each other."

Ms. Douglas' head nodded slightly. Virgil continued his questioning. "Who'd want to kidnap a street kid? No one will pay ransom for you if you're living on the street, right?"

Walker kept her eyes open. *Focus. Stay in the now. Focus. Hold it together.* "That's not why kids get snatched off the streets." Images passed before her eyes. She breathed slowly. *Stay in the now. You're with Ms. Douglas in her kitchen. Safe. You're safe. No one can touch you.*

Virgil demanded, "Why? What does anyone want with a street rat?" He leaned forward, his eyes piercing hers.

Ms. Douglas' voice sliced into the conversation. "Enough, Virgil. Look up the word nefarious. You'll have your answer."

Walker jumped to her feet. "May I help you fix dinner?"

"It's all done, young woman." Ms. Douglas smiled.

Walker insisted. "Then let me set the table. I need to do something." She held the principal's eyes. And held them. And held them.

Ms. Douglas nodded. "Fine. Dishes are in the cabinet." She pointed out which one. "Silverware is in the top drawer under the instant pot. I'll get out the napkins." She ordered, "You boys, go drape yourselves somewhere else. I'll call you when dinner's ready."

Virgil and Larl got up. The boys moseyed to the back, presumably to Larl's bedroom. Walker lowered her head. "Thank you."

Ms. Douglas shrugged. "Boy was asking too many questions that weren't his business. I apologize for him."

Walker shook her head. "No need." She shrugged. "It's still too close."

"I understand." Ms. Douglas sat at the table as Walker set the plates and silverware out for four. "Life can be hard and cruel."

Walker focused on the task in front of her. She waited until she had control of her voice to answer. "Yes, it can." She glanced up at Ms. Douglas. "Takes purpose to pull you out."

"Agreed. I can tell you found yours."

Walker nodded. "Not aggravating Brother Matt is a good one."

The older woman smiled. "True.

~

Dinner over, table cleared, and the Willis's still hadn't arrived. Larl suggested, "How about a game of Horse? That's non-contact. Mom, you shoot too. You're good at it."

Ms. Douglas shrugged. "Yeah, why not? It's been a while since I've put you in your place."

Larl laughed. "You're right." He turned to Walker. "You do know how to play, right?"

"I have to make the same shot you do, or I get a letter. First one to get Horse loses. I know the game."

"Good. Let's go."

Virgil flipped the lights on out back where the court stood. Walker nodded. Full court in the backyard. Larl took his sport seriously. With his mom's approval, no doubt. *Wonder what it would feel like to have the support of a family?*

Wonder what it would feel like to have a family, period.

You had one.

Let's not go there, okay?

Walker stepped out on the court to wait. Ms. Douglas changed her shoes, then came out. "I go first. I'm the oldest."

She shot from the top of the key. Swish. Larl shot, then Virgil. Walker finished the rotation. Ms. Douglas moved directly under the basket. She looped the ball up over the rim. Two points. Everyone followed. The game continued. There were misses, there were (friendly) disputes, there were letters assigned.

No loser or winner had been declared by seven p.m. when Patricia Willis called to say she would be there in five minutes to take Walker back to her people.

Walker smiled at Ms. Douglas. "Thank you for dinner. It was delicious. Thank you for everything. I had a wonderful evening."

She grinned at Larl. "You have a great mom. I hope you appreciate her."

Larl tossed Ms. Douglas the ball. "I do. She won't let me forget how great she is."

Virgil caught hold of Walker's hand. "Hey, before you go…"

Walker froze. She pulled on reserves she prayed she had, then turned to face Virgil. "Please let go of my hand."

He continued to hold it. "No, I just wanted to say I enjoyed playing ball with you. You're really good."

Walker repeated. "Please. Let go of my hand."

Virgil linked his fingers with hers. "What, another of your rules? You're not allowed to touch anyone, either?"

Walker kept tight control of her emotions and her voice. She spaced her words. "Virgil, let go of my hand now."

Ms. Douglas stepped towards Virgil. "Let her go."

Virgil swung her hand with his playfully. "But I like holding your hand."

Walker waited. On the backswing, she twisted his hand and arm behind his back. She pulled it up tight to his shoulder. Virgil yelped.

"Hey! That hurts."

Walker breathed slowly. "I asked you to let go. Do we understand each other?"

Virgil protested, "I was only playing!"

"I'm not." Walker dropped Virgil's arm. She dipped her head to Ms. Douglas. "I apologize. I'm sorry for ending the evening on a bad note."

Ms. Douglas smiled. Her eyes twinkled. "No means no. Men need to learn that." She directed her gaze at Virgil. "Maybe the next time a woman says no, you'll remember."

He rubbed his shoulder. "I'll remember." He shrugged. "Sorry, Walker. I didn't mean anything by it."

Walker nodded. "I'm sorry too. I don't like being held against my will."

The Willis's car pulled into the driveway. Walker started to open the back door. Patricia sat alone behind the wheel, and instructed her, "Come sit up front. It's you and me."

Walker changed positions. "What happened with Mr. Willis?"

"Greg's still at the office. He asked if I would mind taking you back to your encampment alone." She dipped her head. "I wish he'd called me sooner. I would have gotten you home earlier."

Walker smiled. "I'm putting you to a lot of trouble. I can have my team bring me to school, then pick me up at the end of the day. You shouldn't have to do all this running around."

Patricia shook her head. "It's not a problem, honest. We live near the school, and I'm usually swinging by the old church anyhow. I don't know what Greg is working on tonight that's keeping him so late. He's usually home by five."

Walker shrugged. "I had a good time with Ms. Douglas and her son."

"I saw Virgil there, too. He's a wonderful young man." She grinned. "You two would make a good couple if you were staying around longer." Her eyes twinkled. She turned and focused on the road ahead.

Walker stared out the front window. "We have to go back to Oakton. We've all got classes to finish." *Staying would be fun. Not for Virgil. But teaching roundball? A job teaching basketball would make it worth living in a small town. I could like it here.*

A deadly voice hissed in her memory. *"If you ever set foot in this state, I will find you, and I will kill you. Do I make myself clear?"* If the words didn't, the beating did. Walker turned to face out the side window. She closed her eyes and cleared the images from her present. Past. They were all in the past. Let them stay there.

Patricia nodded, unaware of any turmoil in Walker. "I hear you. Still, maybe you could visit after we get rebuilt. You could see what the town is supposed to look like."

Walker smiled. "That would be fun." She turned to stare out the window at the cul-de-sac as they passed. "I still need to examine the place. Chief Zachary asked me to check for signs of arson. I've done everything on the south end except that house. I need to check the ones with fire damage on the north end."

Patricia turned her head to Walker, then turned back to watch the road. "I didn't know you were doing that. Chief Zachary asked you to inspect the place? For arson?"

Walker nodded. "Yes. We found evidence of arson in one building. He wanted me to check all the others before we tore them down. I haven't been able to get to the one here."

"I'm surprised he's asked you to check out the Maugham house. Five people died there. I'm sure someone is investigating it."

Walker's eyes narrowed. "Chief Zachary hasn't said anything. I'll check with him tomorrow about it."

They made small talk the remainder of the way to the camp. Once they arrived, Walker slid out. Patricia insisted, "I'll pick you up in the morning and take you to school. It's the least we can do for you. Having you cover the girls' class means more than you can know." She smiled. "We'll make sure you get home in a timely fashion tomorrow."

Walker smiled. "Thank you again. I'll see you in the morning."

She watched Mrs. Willis drive off, then went into the tent.

The group sat together, listening to Ron deliver a devotion. He looked up as Walker entered. The team leader called, "Nice you could join us again. We're almost finished here."

"I'm sorry, Ron. We'll talk when you're through." Walker took a seat on the ground by the opening of the tent. She needed to process the evening. Something felt off. What was going on with the Maugham house?

The first night they hadn't been organized enough to visit. The next night, she had a dresser dropped on her before she could check it out. Then Bobby punched her in the eye. The very next day, she gets pulled out to teach basketball. But she didn't get picked up or brought home until after dark. Even though the Willis's said they would bring her back. Insisted they would. Which gave Walker no chance to check out the burned-out house.

Could this be a deliberate diversion? An attempt to keep her away from the place? Was she building a crisis that didn't exist?

Ron would help her sort it out. Ron would know. She hoped.

The man finished his teaching, then ambled over to sit beside her. He took a place on the ground, crossed his legs in front of him, and stared at her. "Okay, talk. How did the day go? What did you do? Why so late getting home?"

Walker stared at the ground. "Do you think it's strange they would ask me to teach a class? Out of the blue, here, teach this class. 'We don't know anything about you except you can play roundball. That qualifies you. Come on in.'" She raised her head. "I mean, doesn't it seem weird?"

Ron shrugged. "Yeah, it's weird. Except with all the damage and so many people out, it might make sense." He stopped. "In a desperate kind of way, maybe."

"But surely they have a roster of substitute teachers, right? They can't all be unable to work. Why not pull someone from Bell? They didn't get hit by a tornado."

Ron stared at the ground, then looked up at Walker. "I don't know. What bothers you about this?"

"The Maugham house. The house in the cul-de-sac that burned. Five people died. I've been trying for three days now to check it for arson. But something always gets in the way. I get a dresser dropped on me. The same man who was near the dresser is the same one who elbowed me in the eye the next day. The next day after, the coach of Bobby's team comes to me, picks me up, volunteers me to teach at the school. They were supposed to bring me home immediately after, but he got hung up at the office. I don't get home until it's too late to go. I kept telling them I'd call you, but no one would hear of it."

She pursed her lips. "Mrs. Willis seemed confused her husband waited until almost seven to call and tell her to pick me up by herself. I don't think she's involved." She ducked her head to the side. "I don't think Ms. Douglas, the principal, is involved, either. But I've got a bad feeling about Mr. Willis and his basketball team."

"All of them?" Ron's eyebrows rose. Three men of the group passed on the way to the makeshift showers.

Walker shook her head. "I don't know the whole team. I've met Virgil, Larl, and Bobby, of course. Larl is Ms. Douglas' son. I think he's okay. But Virgil…" She shook her head. "He almost got me going asking questions about what it's like on the streets. Why would we worry about whether someone checked in or not? What would anyone want with a street rat?"

Walker pushed ahead. She would not linger. She would not give a breakdown time to develop. "Later, he took my hand and wouldn't let go."

Ron shook his head. "Bad move. Bad move."

Walker nodded. "Yeah. I asked him, I told him, then I showed him." She shrugged. "When his elbow reached his shoulder blade, he got the message."

"I hope he remembers it."

"So do I."

Ron scribbled in the dirt with his finger. He turned away from

Walker, staring out the opening in the tent. "So, they're going to pick you up and take you back to the school again tomorrow?"

"And through the rest of the week."

"School gets out what time?"

"Three-thirty. The girls want to practice after school. The gym stays open until six."

Ron narrowed his eyes, chewed his lower lip, then nodded. "We'll pick you up at the school at six. After, we'll go inspect the house. All of us."

Walker shook her head. "If there's something someone is trying to hide, I don't want to endanger everyone."

"If someone's trying to keep you from exploring it, they won't be nearly as likely to hinder you when there's twenty-five of us there."

Walker rolled the idea around her head. "Makes sense. Okay, we'll do it that way. No more delays. Tomorrow we go."

She stuck her hand out to shake Ron's. He eyed her sideways. She nodded. He took her hand and shook it. Released it quickly. Walker laughed. "I don't mind when I initiate contact. I don't mind incidental contact. I don't like being restrained."

"I understand." Ron made sure not to clap her on the shoulders, she noticed.

He understands, alright. You're liable to go off on him. He knows better.

How can he when I don't?

Walker walked to her cot and stretched out. She kept her prayers soft. "Lord, I don't know what You want from me. I don't know what You expect with Carly. Or with Virgil. Or Larl. Show me what You want me to do. I want to please You, Father. I want You to smile and say well done. I want You to use me. Help me. Please."

You want to please Him? Do more. Work more. Give more. It's all about more. You never do enough. You can do more, you don't want to. He knows it. He'll always know it.

Walker turned her face from the accuser, closed her eyes, and slept.

TUESDAY

Tuesday was a mirror of Monday as far as Walker was concerned. She taught the girls to run, dribble the ball with either hand, to pass, to shoot... She taught the rules—spoken or un—and what sportsmanship looked like. She immersed herself in the experience. Walker hung out in the gym at lunch to work on her game. She practiced everything she taught the girls. Running. Shooting. Dribbling. Anything for an edge. She texted Mrs. Willis to tell her the relief team would pick her up after practice. No problem for them, honest.

After the dismissal bell rang, Walker waited to see who or how many would show up to form teams. Twenty girls drifted into the gym. Walker split them into four groups of five. She set them to play against each other. She rotated people in and out, watching for the strongest players, pairing them with weaker ones. Dynamics. That's what she wanted. Team dynamics. Who could work with who. And how well.

~

Cheering from the bleachers brought her out of her head. Walker came back to the present. She glanced up quickly. A crowd of other young people watched the workouts. The cheers were for a goal scored. Walker had missed the growing audience. She shook her head, checked the time, then blew her whistle. "Good job, players. Hit the showers. Go home. We'll pick it up tomorrow. I'm proud of all of you."

Carly sidled up beside Walker. "Did you even see anyone come in?"

Walker grinned. "Nope. I concentrate too much on the game."

Virgil and Larl stood in the circle driveway when Walker and Carly exited the building. Larl addressed the younger woman. "Hey, May. Very impressive. I didn't know you could play like that."

Carly's jaw fell open. "How did you see me?"

Larl shrugged over his shoulder. "We were watching from the driveway. The doors were open, and we could see you running back and forth. You had some good moves."

A teen passing by sneered, "I'd like to see those moves sometime."

Carly's eyes narrowed to slits. She started after the boy, but Walker warned her off. "Ignore it. Let it go. Prove yourself on the court. That's where the battle is."

Virgil chuckled. "Yeah. Walker should know." Another young man, maybe college-age, walked up to join the group. Carly acknowledged him with a nod.

Walker tipped her head to the side to study Virgil. "Excuse me?"

Virgil held up a hand in defense. "I just mean you let your roundball skills speak for themselves." He smiled. "I want to apologize again for last night. I didn't mean anything by holding your hand."

Walker shrugged. "I forgave you last night. It's over."

He smiled. "Good. You'll come out with me in a group of people tonight?"

"No." Walker shook her head. "My team is picking me up. They should be here any minute. We've got work to do in the field."

"What work? You can't work all day and all night too."

Walker noted the newcomer step closer to her. Tall. Well-built. A serious athlete. She held her ground. "We're not. We have other work than teardowns. We're completing schoolwork and doing prep for Sunday lessons."

"Sunday? What lessons do you have on Sundays?" Virgil sounded incredulous.

Carly laughed. "Don't you know? She's a Jesus Freak." Carly smiled at Walker. "Sorry, Jesus follower."

Do not react. Smile and say, "Yes, I am."

"Yes, I am." Walker looked around for the bus and her team.

The young man drew another step closer. His eyes narrowed. He looked from Carly to Walker. "She's part of a cult?"

Walker shrugged. "Call it a cult if you like. I call it living the way Jesus would." She stepped around him. "Now, if you'll excuse me—"

The boy stepped in Walker's way. "Does Coach Willis know you're part of a cult?"

Larl punched the boy in the shoulder. "Knock it off, Jim. You don't know what you're talking about." Jim ignored Larl, his eyes laser-focused on Walker.

Walker kept her eyes on Jim. "If Coach Willis has spoken to Pastor Mars, who invited us here, I'm sure he knows what we believe. And what we practice."

Jim's eyes flashed. "I don't like the idea of someone coming in here teaching school kids strange ideas." His fists clenched. His jaw tightened.

Walker kept her tone smooth. "I wouldn't either. Except I haven't taught anyone anything except basketball. If you have firsthand knowledge of me teaching anything else, you'll need to take it up with Ms. Douglas."

Walker moved to pass Jim by, but he blocked her path. He glared down at her. "I don't trust you here. Not in this school. Not in this town. I don't need outsiders teaching my sister weird religious ideas."

Carly jumped into the argument. "She's not teaching me anything, Jim. She's teaching us basketball. What's got into you?"

He continued to stare down at Walker. "I suggest you take your team and get out of town tonight. You've been warned. You hear me?" He caught hold of her arm, then jerked her around.

Virgil lowered his head and shook it. "Bad move, Jim. Bad move." He stepped out of Jim's way.

Walker lifted her chin. "Let go of my arm." She didn't bother with please.

Jim squeezed hard. "What are you going to do about it?"

The challenge was clear. *No one is going to come to your defense. Everyone wants to see if you'll fight back. It's a game.*

Walker repeated. "Let go of my arm, or I will be forced to put you on the floor, step over you, then report you for assault and battery."

He glared at her. "You're all mouth. I'm the one holding you." He twisted her arm for emphasis.

Walker held his eyes. "Let go." She spaced the words. So, there could be no mistake.

Virgil warned, "Do it, Jim. Let go of her. Unless you want your arm broken."

Carly yelled, "Jim! What's with you? Let her go!" Carly pulled at her brother's arm. He jerked it back, nearly knocking Carly to the floor.

Larl added to the uproar. "Get off her!"

Jim dropped her arm. Walker moved past him. He grabbed her from behind. She stepped back into him, caught his arm, spun him around to the floor. Jim scrambled to his feet and came after her again. Walker sidestepped his charge, letting him run past her.

He whirled to come back at her. Jim grabbed her arms. Walker curled a leg around his knee and brought him to the ground. She swung to her feet. Jim clutched at her legs. Walker danced away. The man rolled to his feet and came after her again…

Then froze as Ms. Douglas thundered, "Enough! James!"

The principal walked up to the warring parties. "What's going on here?"

"She attacked me!" Jim breathed hard and heavy, trying to catch his breath.

Walker said nothing. She stood, waiting quietly. She barely breathed. Virgil and Larl both jumped in. "No, she didn't. He grabbed her."

"Everyone, my office. Now."

Ms. Douglas eyed Walker. "You'll need to tell your team you'll be delayed a while. I'll make this as fast as I can. But we have rules to follow."

Walker nodded. "I understand." *I understand more than you know. Someone set this up. Very neat trap.*

Because it had been a dispute on school grounds, the police had to be called. Everyone had to be interviewed separately. Any witnesses had to be rounded up. They had to tell their stories. After two hours, the police decided Jim was at fault. Since he wasn't a student at the school, the rules about teachers not laying hands on a student didn't apply. Had he been, self-defense or not, Walker would have been escorted off the property in handcuffs.

Ms. Douglas stared down the officer who threatened Walker. She tapped her foot slowly. "The day my teachers can't defend themselves against being attacked by anyone is the day I turn in my resignation. If Jim were a student here, she would still have had every right to fight back. I'll stand with my people every time."

The officer tipped his hat. "I understand, Ms. Douglas. I didn't write the rules."

"I'm sure you didn't. But you let it be known to those who did. My school will never be a hunting ground against the teachers." Ms. Douglas slapped her hand on her desk.

"Yes, ma'am." He backed out of the door and left.

Ms. Douglas sighed. "I am sorry, Walker. I have no idea what got into the boy. It's ridiculous. Holding you up like this? When three people saw exactly what happened and told the truth about it?"

She shook her head. "I've been here too long." The principal dropped her head to her desk.

Walker smiled at her. "Don't quit. These kids need you. Too many good ones are left for a bad apple to run you off." *This was a setup, anyhow.*

Ms. Douglas sighed. "I hope you're right. I'm getting too old for these games." She sat up, then waved Walker off with the back of her hand. "Go home. I'll see you in the morning." She smiled. "Stay out of trouble. If you can."

"Yes, ma'am. I'm trying."

Walker turned and hustled to the parking lot where the team bus waited. Ron cranked the engine when she approached. As she climbed on board, the team all cheered. Walker ducked her head to the side. "Knock it off. If I'd got fired, you'd all be stuck with me. Again."

Maria laughed. "Aw, you know we love you." She patted the seat beside her. Walker sat on the bench with her.

Ron put the bus in motion. He looked in the rearview mirror. "What happened?"

Walker gave him a fast run-down of the setup fight. "I've seen people pick phony fights, but this was ridiculous. Calling us a cult? Come on. All he wanted to do was keep me at school."

Ron grimaced. "He did it well, didn't he? Is he another one of Coach Willis' recruits?" He gunned the bus around the corner.

Walker ran the episode through her memory, placing the players in their spots. "He came with Virgil and Larl, so I'm guessing so."

Ron pulled into the cul-de-sac. The streetlight had been put out. No illumination at all. "This is a bust. Again."

Walker scowled. "Right. Five days running. Someone really doesn't want me to investigate it." Her fists tightened. So did her resolve. She would investigate. No one would stop her. The Lord brought her here for this. She would not let Him down.

"I think it's time to call Chief Zachary and let him know. I realize he's over in another town, but he may need to step in here." Ron turned the bus down the street and headed to their camp.

"Agreed." Walker stared at the floor of the bus. "I wonder what the police are doing about this? You'd think they'd do autopsies. Something, anyhow."

"I'd let the chief make those inquiries. After tonight, who knows what stories will get spread?" Ron's face reflected disgust. Tinged with concern.

Walker lifted her head. "You think this is going to blow up into something more? He got what he wanted. We were delayed past dark." *Did I blow our witness? Forgive me, Lord. I'm sorry. I never intended to interfere with Your work.*

Ron shrugged. "Maybe. Maybe it goes deeper." He turned the bus down the street to the former church. "I think we should be prepared…"

A loud bang sounded from under the bus. Ron swerved but maintained control. He pulled the vehicle over. Everyone peered out to see what had happened.

The front tire had blown out. Ron groaned. "Great." He glanced around. "Alright, guys. We all know how to change a tire. Get the jack, the lug wrench, and the spare."

Four of the men began pulling items from under the back seat. Jun called, "Ron, the spare is flat."

"What?" Ron jumped in the aisle to see. "It was good when we left Oakton."

"It has no air in it." Jun pushed down on the tire to show it had no air.

Tyler rummaged through the toolbox. "Lug wrench is missing, too." He turned to glance at Ron.

Ron snarled. "I made sure to put it in there. I did it myself."

"You search. I can't find it." Tyler shoved the box at Ron.

Ron sat back on his haunches. "I believe you." He scowled. "Get the jack." He stopped. "Is it still there?"

Jun pulled the hydraulic jack from under a seat mid-way up the aisle. "It's here. They probably didn't have time to search for it."

Ron huffed. "I want to examine the tire. I want to see if I can tell what happened. Maybe it'll be an easy fix."

Walker climbed out of the bus with the other students. She withdrew into a shell. *Deliberate. This was deliberate.*

Of course. It's all your fault. You had to show off to the pastor. "Look at me. I'm soooo smart." See what trouble you brought to the team?

The men grunted, groaned, and eventually lifted the bus off the ground in the front. Ron lay on the ground, rotating the tire searching for the hole. After a thorough search, he stood, brushed off his clothes, and glanced around. "There's a hole the size of a nickel in one side and out the other. Someone shot our tire."

A buzz of voices. "What are we going to do?" "Why?" "What now?"

Ron waved everyone down. He lowered his head. "Lord, thank You, no one got hurt. We don't know who did this or what they intended. But we're in Your hands. This didn't surprise You. Tell us what to do. How do we bring You glory in this? Keep us in Your will, Father." He looked up. "I'll call the road service. If the spare is only flat, we'll be back in business in another hour. If it's damaged, too, we'll be here longer." He retrieved his phone. "Maybe they have a matching tire lying around."

Your fault. All this is your fault. You hurt everyone who cares about you. You defile everything you touch.

Maria touched Walker's arm. "Stop." Walker jerked. "Stop blaming yourself. This isn't you. It's the enemy. He's after all of us." She smiled gently.

Walker breathed out slowly. She nodded. "I hear you."

"Good. Now, believe me." Maria grinned.

Walker ducked her head. "Gotcha." *Why does everyone say that?*

Ron announced, "There will be a tow truck here in half an hour. The driver thinks he has a spare that will match." He circled with his finger. "Dig deep, people. He only takes cash."

Groans and catcalls met him. But hands reached into pockets and bags. Before long, Ron had a wad of cash. "This should be enough."

Jun quipped, "If it is not, I need to change careers."

Ben punched him in the arm. "You and me both."

The group waited patiently. Maria began an acapella version of a praise hymn. Voices joined. Four-part harmony lifted to the heavens above. Walker breathed in deeply. *Thank You, Lord. Thank You for my sister. She keeps me grounded in You. I want to say I love her, but I still don't know what loving someone is like. People who love me die. I don't want to kill anyone else.*

You have killed no one.

She's killed everyone. She's death. She knows it.

Walker lifted her head to join the singing. It closed out the accusations. And the memories.

Half an hour later, the tow truck arrived. The driver checked the group's spare and found a slit in the sidewall. He did have a tire that would work, however. Fifteen minutes of manual labor followed. The bus resumed its trip home. Without further incident.

No insulting banter pressed Walker as she went to her cot. Had Ron threatened the group? It wouldn't be the first time he'd disciplined this motley crew before the fact. She appreciated being the recipient of the team's grace. If she could only figure out how to extend it to herself...

Lights out followed shortly. Walker stared at the darkness, unable to sleep. *How do I get to the house without endangering anyone else? How do I keep the team safe?*

She remained stock still. No tossing and turning to alert the others she couldn't sleep. No tells. Her problem. Hers alone. Involve no one...

Maria whispered, "Walker, I have an idea."

"What?"

"In the morning, right after sunup, we'll take the bus and go to the house. We can be there and back before your ride comes to take you to work.”

“I don't want to—”

“Do you want to inspect it or not?”

“Yes, but—”

“We're doing it.” Maria's voice shifted. She'd rolled from her side to her back.

“You could get hurt.” Walker rolled toward her friend.

“So could you.”

“But I've been asked to do this. You haven't.”

“I'm very sure Chief Zachary would not have asked you to do something if he had any idea you would be in danger.” Maria's voice shifted again.

“It doesn't matter. He asked, so I have to do it.”

“Says who? The tyrant in your head?” Walker didn't answer. “That's what I thought. He doesn't own you, Walker. Not anymore. Let him go. No one expects you to walk into a dangerous situation. If it's too dangerous for me to go, it's too dangerous for you. Accept it. Believe it. We go together, or neither of us goes.”

Walker closed her eyes.

Listen to her. She speaks the truth.

She has no clue what's required of you. You were given the job. God knew it, so God ordered it. You can't let God down. You have to go.

If I knew how to drive the bus...

You don't. Ron has the keys. Maria isn't serious about going. She's trying to give you a cover for your cowardice.

Walker bowed her head. *Father, help me. Tell me what You want me to do. Did you put me here to do this? Or am I supposed to be learning how not to be a martyr? Help me know the difference.*

The voices would argue deep into the night. There would be no resolution.

WEDNESDAY

Wednesday morning, Walker opened her eyes. Maria rolled over and grinned at her. "You're still here."

Walker scowled at her. "Yes, I'm still here. Couldn't figure a way to sneak off without you."

Maria eyed her. "Is that the only reason you're still here?"

Walker lowered her eyes. "No. The Lord and I couldn't come to an agreement about what I should do. I wanted to leave, but that wasn't the right answer. Not without being sure."

Maria stretched. "You're learning. Waiting on Him can be hard. But it's always the right answer." The woman leaned forward to touch her toes. Twice.

Walker grimaced. "Except when it's not. If I remember correctly, He told Moses to stop crying and start moving." Walker fought with her blanket, trying to get the unruly fabric to let go of her.

"Different situation." Maria climbed from her bunk and grabbed a towel. "Let's hit the showers before the men use all the hot water."

"Good thought." Walker threw the blanket down on the bottom of the cot. She followed Maria out into the cool morning air.

No one stirred in the encampment. The sun peeked above the rolling hills, tinting the sky a brilliant fiery pink. Clouds melted away from the horizon. A mockingbird called the world to life. Walker breathed in the freshness of the day. Seeing the day begin again gave her peace. Whatever the Lord had for her, it would be good. Good, and for her good. She would face life today. One day at a time.

Showers over, the two women walked back to the cook area. Maria pulled out supplies to make pancakes. She instructed Walker how to tell if the batter was thick enough, the griddle hot enough, when the pancake would be ready to flip.

Walker followed the directions with precision. She stacked pancakes in the oven to keep them warm. Breakfast would be waiting when the rest of the team rose. *It's the least I can do for them.*

Yeah. You always do the least you can do.

Walker ignored the taunt. He would not own her today. Today, she belonged to the Lord.

We'll see. We will see.

Maria and Walker enjoyed their breakfast before the others rose. When the team straggled out of their slumbers, Maria and Walker served them the still-warm pancakes.

Ron stuffed his mouth with flapjacks and syrup, then came to sit beside Walker and Maria. He swallowed. "Why don't we go to the house on the cul-de-sac? We could take pictures for you. It wouldn't tell you everything, but maybe it's a start. Maybe it shows there's nothing to be concerned about."

Walker shook her head. "Someone shot at the bus when we were just driving by there. What do you think would happen if you actually stopped to take pictures? I don't think exposing the whole team is a good idea."

"You think leaving it for Chief Zachary is a better plan?" Ron pulled another flapjack from the pile and slathered it with butter. He cut it into pieces and stabbed a forkful.

Walker fought to answer. After several moments she nodded. "Yes. Will you call him? It's too early now. I may not have time later in the day." She finished her plate, spooning up all the syrup without actually licking the plate.

Ron nodded. "Sure." He smiled at her. "Very wise of you to call in the professional."

Walker shook her head. "It goes against everything inside me. I should be the one doing it, not leaving it for someone else to cover." She shoved her used plate into the trash receptacle. If only she could dispose of her guilt as well.

Ron put his plate down. "It wasn't your responsibility to begin with. We're here to help, not solve all the town's problems." He held Walker in his gaze. "I think Brother Matt gave you that specific instruction, didn't he? What did he make you repeat before you got on the bus?"

Walker grimaced. "It is not my responsibility to save this town from their distress. I can help, but it is not my job to carry the entire burden." Her eyes narrowed. "But if the Lord has asked me to do something, shouldn't I be doing it, not leaving it to someone else?" She tipped her head. "If He put me here for a purpose, aren't I failing Him when I don't complete it?"

Ron shook his head. "Maybe your only purpose was to find the church arson. You found it. Now that's the end of it." He emptied his breakfast into his mouth, then threw the plate away.

The Willis's' silver sedan pulled into the parking lot. Walker held up her hand to Ron. "Hold that thought. We'll come back to it tonight."

"We will pick you up at six." Ron grinned. "Try to stay out of trouble."

Walker snorted. "Believe me, I will." She walked up the hill to the car.

Patricia smiled at her as Walker slid into the shotgun seat. "Good morning! I hope you had a good evening with your team."

Walker closed the door. Tell? Don't tell? Did the woman already know? Walker debated, then said, "It was eventful. Jim Davies accused me of bringing cult doctrines to the girls I'm teaching. He grabbed my arm. I got it back. He attacked me. I defended myself. The police came. Since he's not a student at the school, they didn't arrest me."

Patricia's mouth hung open. "What? He did what? Why?"

Walker nodded. "He told the police I threw the first punch, but there were four people, including Ms. Douglas, as witnesses. We all finally got let go about eight." She decided to tell the rest of the story as well. "Someone shot a hole in the front tire of the bus on the way home."

Patricia stared at Walker, then returned to watch the road in front of her. "Someone shot a hole in your tire? Why? I don't understand."

Walker shrugged. "I have a theory. I think I'm being deliberately detained." She admitted, "The flat tire was a setup. Whoever planned it stole the tools we needed to put on the spare. They even cut the spare so it couldn't be used." She gazed at Patricia. "I feel like someone doesn't want me to finish the work Chief Zachary gave me."

They rode in silence for a few blocks. Patricia asked, "So what houses are you still investigating?"

"I'm done with everything on the south end except the Maugham house." She eyed Patricia. "That's where we were when someone shot the bus."

Patricia's eyes puddled. "We lost a good family there. All four of them."

Walker narrowed her eyes. "There were five people killed."

Patricia shook her head. "I keep hearing that, but I can't imagine who the fifth person could be. Jill didn't say anything about having company. It's not like either of them had family who would drop in. Something's not right about it."

She glanced at Walker, then back to her driving. "I asked Greg, and he said I shouldn't worry about it. Once the police do their investigation, it will all be figured out."

Walker probed, "Has there been a coroner's report?"

"No. The coroner's been out of state for a month now. I'm not sure where he is, but Greg says he won't be back for another two weeks or so. There's no one else who can do the autopsies." Patricia shook her head as she turned the car into the circle drive of the school. "It's not right. I know that much. It's not right."

Walker tried to smile at the distraught woman. "The Lord has it, Mrs. Willis. I don't always know what He's doing, but I'm learning He is moving."

Patricia smiled. "I love your faith, Walker. You sure you don't need a ride home?"

"No, I'll be fine. I promised my team leader I'd stay out of trouble. He promised to pick me up. But thank you. Have a good day."

Walker opened the door, slid out of the car, then closed the door. She walked into the building and headed directly to Ms. Douglas' office. The older woman sat with her hands folded on her desk. "Ms. Walker." Piles of clipboards sat on the corner of the desk. A frightened student sat in the anteroom.

"Ms. Douglas. I promised my team leader I would stay out of trouble. I'm promising you the same thing." Walker stood straight.

Ms. Douglas pursed her lips. "I think the trouble is finding you. The whole incident last night was uncalled for." She tapped her fingers on the top of her desk. "I've been rolling it over and over in my head, trying to make it make sense. It doesn't." She stared at Walker. "Please be careful today."

Walker nodded. "I will." She hesitated, then pushed the door closed. "Someone shot at our bus last night. Shot out the front tire. Someone else sabotaged the spare tire, so we couldn't put it on. We had to call roadside assistance. Cost us dearly." May as well tell her the rest. "I think it has to do with the Maugham house. I'm supposed to check it for signs of arson, but something always gets in the way."

Ms. Douglas shook her head. "Even more reason to be careful." She stood. "I'll keep my eyes open. You should too."

Walker ducked her head. "I will."

She turned, opened the door, walked to the gym for her first class. Ms. Douglas called, "Serena. I will see you now." *Poor Serena.*

~

First period, second period, third period…the day went by. Nothing disturbed the classes or Walker's teaching. She took five minutes at lunch to call Ron but only got his voicemail. She tried Maria's cell but got the same result. Not surprising. The team usually had their phones on silent while in the field. Be present where you are.

The day ended with no incidents. Girls filed in for team practice. Walker divided them up into different groups and set them to work. Run, pass, dribble. Run, dribble, pass. Shooting came last. She had the girls practicing from the free-throw line. "Five in a row. Muscle memory. Hit the same spot every time."

Walker moved amongst them, watching, encouraging, coaching… The last fifteen minutes of the hour, the girls got to scrimmage a real game. Ten girls on the floor. The rest rotating in and out at a moment's notice. No time outs, no breaks. Walker called two names, and the girls would switch. She watched them all with a critical eye. Who made the strongest team? Maybe not the best individual players, but who had the chemistry to play together?

At six, she blew the whistle. "Time. Hit the showers and go home. You did good. I'm proud of all of you."

Carly raised her hand. "Have you decided on who's your starting line-up?"

Walker smiled. "Still working on it. I'm getting close. We've got tomorrow and Friday, then Saturday, we scrimmage for Ms. Douglas."

"Then she lets us be an intramural team."

"If we prove ourselves. One day at a time, Carly."

The girl waited until the other players had dispersed. She came close to Walker. "I want to apologize for what my brother did yesterday. He was stupid. I don't understand it."

Walker shrugged. "Yeah, I don't understand it, either. But you didn't have anything to do with it, so no apology necessary." She stuffed the basketballs in their container.

"Mom reamed him out good when he got home. After you saved Alissa, he wants to cause you trouble? She had a fit." Carly sat on the bleacher to watch Walker.

Walker shook her head. "I'm sorry it happened. He must have heard something somewhere, and it hit him wrong. Don't hold it against him. I don't." She waved a hand to show it meant nothing.

"Of course, you don't. You're a Jesus Freak. You guys forgive everything, right?"

Walker looked outside but didn't see the bus. She sat on the bleacher beside the girl. "We try, Carly. We don't get it perfect. God forgave us. We're supposed to live like Him." She buried any attempt from the past to break through into her memory. *Not here. Not now. You don't own me.*

I own everything about you. I made you. I can unmake you.

Walker closed her eyes. "It's a process. We learn, we grow. We give Him our lives all in a moment, then spend the rest of time giving it back to Him piece by piece."

Carly snorted. "Right. There's nothing God can't forgive, right? It doesn't matter what you do. 'Poof,' you're forgiven." The sarcasm and ridicule in her voice came through loud and clear.

Walker breathed in slowly. "Does it matter? Yes, it does. Will He forgive? Yes. Are there consequences? Yes."

Carly tipped her head. "Yeah? Like what?"

"Like if you've been a thief, you need to make restitution. If you've harmed someone, you need to make it right. You need to make amends." Walker chewed the inside of her cheek. She could feel her hands beginning to tremble. No one would see it, but she felt it. "If you've committed crimes, you need to confess. There might be jail time. There might be probation. It doesn't matter. You need to make it right."

Carly eyed her closely. "You're talking about you, aren't you?"

Walker lifted her chin. "I lived on the streets, Carly. Survived on the streets. I'm sure you can imagine what that might require. Brother Golding took me in and introduced me to Jesus. When I finally accepted Him, I knew I had to clean up my act. Part of it meant making restitution where I could. Some of it, I can't." She looked at the floor. "But by God's grace and Brother Matt's help, I did what I could."

Walker gazed at Carly. "That's why I volunteer at the center. It's my way of giving back. Of trying to help some other kid stay clean and off the street."

"Clean. You mean like from drugs and stuff?"

Walker held Carly's gaze. "Use your imagination. Imagine it as bad as it can get. That's how I lived, Carly. That's what Jesus saved me from. That's what I want to keep other children from experiencing."

"I don't get how you can forgive people for what they did to you. Doesn't it stay with you?"

Walker breathed deep.

Tell her the truth. You've never forgiven him. Never will. Can't. Won't.

I want to.

Not bad enough. If you wanted to, you would. The memories would never bother you again. Right? You'd be free. All the pain would be gone.

No. Brother Matt said it's a process. Something I have to do over and over and over.

So what good is it?

Carly called her name. "Walker. Did you hear me?"

Walker drew herself into her shell. "It stays with you. You don't suddenly forget everything bad that happened to you. But you forgive. Jesus knows who we are. He doesn't hold it against us. I can't hold it against the ones who…" She stopped. Closed her eyes. Drew the shell tighter. "The ones who hurt me."

Images of a man standing over her, beating her, yelling at her, berating her flashed in her mind. Toddler. Youngster. First grade. Second grade. Third grade. Always yelling. Always ranting. Always criticizing. Telling her he did it because he loved her. Love meant pain. Rejection. Abandonment.

Walker opened her eyes. Carly stared at her. Walker's voice trembled. "I'm not perfect, Carly. I'm learning. I'm trying. It's hard. But I'm trying."

Carly shook her head. "I don't think I could ever do that. Not if it were me."

Walker lowered her eyes. "I pray it never is, Carly. You'll have your own need to come to the Savior for forgiveness. We all do. I don't want anyone to follow my path. Ever. Which is why I do what I do."

Carly shrugged. "Yeah, whatever." She bumped Walker with her shoulder. "See you tomorrow, Teacher." Carly rose, grabbed her books, and left the gym.

Walker sat. She stared at the floor. Her tormentors jeered.

You've never forgiven anyone anything. You're a fake. A liar. A cheat.

You can't do it. Not him. You'll never forgive him. Jesus will never forgive you, either. You have to forgive others first, remember? That's what the Bible says. He forgives you as you forgive others. But you won't, so He won't, either. You're doomed. He'll never love you.

I have loved you with an everlasting love. I am with you always.
Not you. Never you. Others. Not you.

Walker gathered her backpack. She walked out to the parking lot. No bus. Walker sank down on the flag stand. She gazed up the street and waited.

Thirty minutes.

Sixty minutes.

Walker checked her phone. Nothing.

Ninety minutes. Still nothing on her phone.

Two hours. The bus pulled around the circle. Ron opened the door. Walker climbed on board. Ron demanded, "Why is your phone off? Maria, Jun, Ben, and I have all tried to call you. We kept getting the message your phone had been turned off."

Walker glared at him as she took a seat behind him. "I never turned it off." She pulled it out to look at it, then held it up for him to see. "It's on. It's been on all day."

"Check the mode." Ron put the bus in motion, drove around the circle, and headed for the encampment.

Walker checked the settings. Wifi was off. Someone had switched her phone to airplane mode. No calls could come in or go out. Her eyes narrowed as she stared at it. She raised her head to stare at Ron. "I swear I had it in regular mode this morning. I never change it. Never."

Ron nodded. "I believe you. But someone switched it." He checked both ways at a railroad crossing. "We were delayed. A gravel truck dumped its load in front of us. We were buried in the stone for almost two hours." He grimaced. "Even with all of us shoveling with our hands, we still couldn't get out of the mess. We tried to call you."

Chills ran up her spine. Her team had been attacked. There was no other way to consider it. Someone had targeted the team. Yeah, maybe whoever meant it as a delaying tactic, but they still directed it at her people. What would the bad guys do next?

Walker covered her mouth with her hand. She sat immobile for several moments. "Did you reach Captain Zachary?"

"He said he was still tied up in Bell. But he said not to worry about the Maugham house. If you get to it, fine. If you don't, it's fine, too. He'll check it when he gets back. You're absolved of responsibility for it."

"Did he say that?" Walker watched Ron's eyes in the mirror. She would know. She always knew.

He nodded. "His exact words: 'I absolve Walker of responsibility for checking the house.' Are you satisfied?"

Walker frowned but agreed. "Yes." Ron wouldn't lie. He might dodge around the truth, but he would not lie. Walker stared out the window, letting the lights and shadows pass in succession. She did not try to sort them out.

Until they passed the cul-de-sac with the Maugham house. She saw a light near the house. Flickering. Growing. Her eyes widened. "Stop! Stop the bus. There's a fire."

Ron slammed the brakes. Grumbles and protests from the back shouted at him. He steered the bus to the side of the road and stopped. Walker jumped out. She raced up the sidewalk to where the flames ate at the base of the house. She stripped her shirt off to begin pounding out the fire.

Ron yelled for the fire extinguisher. Walker stomped the fire with her feet. Battered it with her hands. Smothered it with the shirt. Anything to put the flames out. Someone wanted to destroy evidence. Someone wanted to burn down the remaining house before it could be investigated.

Not on my watch. Not while I can stop them.

Ron shoved her aside. He began spraying foam on the fire. Walker raced to the back and found the bushes below the kitchen window burning. She yelled for Ron but didn't wait. Again, she stomped the flames, digging dirt, throwing it on the shrubs to put them out. She beat the glowing branches with her hands. Nothing mattered but preserving the evidence. Sparks kindled but extinguished in the wet grass.

Ron raced around the back with the extinguisher, accompanied by a group from the bus. Together they stomped the last of the blazing embers.

Sirens called in the distance, growing louder and louder. Fire trucks pulled into the cul-de-sac. A police car accompanied them. The lead fireperson yelled, "Who called in the fire? Where's it at?"

Ron pointed to the bus. "We did. We found it burning around the outside. We haven't checked the inside." Two of the firefighters disappeared into the house.

The door of the police car opened. A large, angry police chief climbed out. He demanded to know, "What's going on? Who set those fires?"

Ron stepped forward. "We saw the bushes on fire when we drove by. We stopped and put them out."

The firefighters returned from checking the house. "All clear inside."

A breeze chilled Walker's back. She ducked behind Ron and hissed, "Give me your shirt."

He turned to look at her. He protested, "It's my lucky Buckeye shirt."

Walker crossed her arms over the front of her. She hissed, "I'm in my underwear. I'll get you another one. Give it to me."

Ron pulled it over his head and handed it to her. It left him in his white undershirt. At least he had something. Which was more than Walker would have had. She donned the shirt, then stepped out from behind him. She took a step toward the police chief but stopped as he glared at her. "You. You're the one causing trouble at the school, aren't you?" He smiled. "Only joking, of course."

Walker cocked her head. "Excuse me, sir?"

"I know who you are. I saw the report from last night. You were involved in a fight with a student, weren't you?" The chief continued to smile.

Walker chose her words carefully. "Not a student from the high school, no, sir." She did not return his smile. Fake smile. The eyes…the eyes never lie. Calm. She would be calm.

"I see you're rescuing us again, aren't you, Miss? We can't do anything without your help. Walker, isn't it?" The smile hardened. But he kept his words, for the record, friendly. He looked around at the house. "Why were you even over here? Your camp is at Pastor Mars' field. Were you trying to find trouble to stop? So you can be more of a hero?" He laughed.

Ron stepped up. "I chose the route home, sir. This is the shortest distance from the school to the camp. We pass this way every night.

We saw the fires burning, stopped, and put them out."

The chief nodded. "Ah, I see. You needed a little more excitement, did you? Get a little boring hauling trash? Finding some other way to get your names in the paper?" He smiled. "Students from the big city have to come down here to show us simple folk how it's done, right?"

Ron's eyes flared, but his voice stayed under control. "All we're doing is hauling trash and debris, sir. Homeowners point to what they want moved. We move it. We're not here to show anyone anything."

The chief raised his eyebrows. "No? Your little girl got Bobby Eller kicked off the team after she decided to show him how to 'play' with her." He made the insinuation clear. The smile remained. The eyes leered.

Walker held her tongue. Ron had this. She would wait on him. He would defend what needed to be defended. If anything.

Ron called, "People, on the bus." The students filed past him, excusing themselves with utmost tact as they moved around the police chief. Ron waited until they were all on. He turned back to the chief. "Sir, Mr. Greg Willis made the decision to remove Bobby from the team. Two of his teammates were present at the time of the incident. They explained the whole matter. There was no impropriety at any time."

The chief eyed Walker. His eyes bored into her. But the smile remained. "That's not what I heard." Friendly. Oh, so friendly.

"I would ask you to speak to Greg Willis. Ms. Douglas was aware of the incident last night. She stated Walker was in no way at fault for the attack on her."

Chief continued to stare at Walker. "Again, that's not what I heard. The story I got was you were teaching the boy's sister ideas from some cult you follow. He objected, and you swung on him."

Ron pulled out his phone. "Sir, we can call Ms. Douglas right now. She'll be happy to straighten this out."

The chief waved his hand as if waving off a fly. "I don't need to talk to her or anyone else. I'm like my townspeople. We draw our conclusions from what we're told." His eyes narrowed. "And by who." He stared directly into Walker's eyes. "So we understand each other, Ms. I don't need trouble. These people don't need trouble. If you want to help, do what you came to do. Carry trash." The chief's smile faded slightly. "If I see you, or hear of you, anywhere else, I'll assume you're causing trouble. I'll have to arrest you for trespassing where you don't belong. Do we understand each other?"

Ron stepped between the chief and Walker. "Are you threatening the entire team? Throwing us all out of town? On what charge, sir?"

The chief smiled. He clapped a heavy hand on Ron's shoulder. "I don't mind if the rest of you stay. I haven't heard a word against any of you." His eyes narrowed as he stared at Walker. "Only her."

Walker touched Ron's arm. He peered at her. She nodded. Ron eyed her. She nodded again. He turned back to the chief. "We will stay out the week we committed to volunteer. Walker will remain with Pastor Mars' family until we're finished. That puts her out of town and out of trouble." He motioned for Walker to get on the bus.

She slid past the police chief. The man caught hold of Walker's arm. Walker froze. *Do not respond. This is a setup. He wants you to swing on him. He's dying for you to react. He's probably heard what happened with Virgil. He wants to see it for himself. Do not respond.*

The chief pulled her around to face him. "If you think saving Ms. Alissa and her baby wins you any credit, it doesn't. She's an outsider. She doesn't belong here. Neither do you. You get no points for being a hero in my book. My book is the only one that counts. Are we clear?"

Walker remained calm. She would not react. The chief squeezed her arm. Ron couldn't see the motion. It was a test. How long would it take before she made a scene? Cried out? Struck out?

The pressure increased. Walker held his eyes. "I understand perfectly, Police Chief Perkins." No reaction. She would not give him the satisfaction.

He squeezed harder. Walker didn't move. She leveled her gaze at him. Held his eyes. His anger burned. Walker continued to stand firm. *I trained for this. You have nothing on the man who taught me never to show pain. This is a picnic.*

Chief Perkins released her arm. "Get out of here." He smiled and waved at the people on the bus. "Have a good night, now."

Walker climbed on the bus. She took a seat behind Ron. Ron took the driver's seat, closed the door, and pulled out onto the road. No one spoke. No one moved.

They pulled into the parking lot at the church. The group dismounted, then gathered in the tent. Lights were turned on. The students sat in a circle on the ground.

Maria touched Walker's arm. "Your hands are burned. Let me take care of them." She led Walker to the basin, where she poured water over Walker's hands.

Walker stopped her. "Wait. I need to take off Ron's shirt. I don't want to get anything on it."

Maria motioned for Walker to sit. "I'll get you one. Wait here." The woman retrieved a short-sleeved shirt from Walker's duffle. Maria handed it to her. Walker shifted out of Ron's pullover and into her own. She laid it aside, then called "Ron. You can have your shirt back. In one piece." Maria went back to doctoring Walker's hands.

Ron walked over and picked it up. He pulled it over his head. "We need to decide what we're going to do." His eyes glazed. He pointed to Walker's arm where the police chief held her. "Did he do that?"

Walker looked down at the angry red and purple start of a bruise. She glanced up at Ron. "Yeah. He wanted to see if I'd come unglued or fight with him like I did with the others. I wouldn't give him the satisfaction."

Ron closed his eyes, turned away from the women, and stood with his fists clenched. His arms trembled. Walker lowered her head. *Lord, help him. Give him strength or whatever he needs to get through this Your way. He wants to bring You honor and glory. We all do. Don't let my actions ruin whatever You're doing with the rest of the team. I'm nothing. They don't need me. You don't need me. Send me home if that's what You need to do. Or take me out. Whatever You know best. But help Ron. And Maria. And Jun. And Ben. And...*

Ron turned around. He breathed deeply. The man relaxed his fists. He pointed to Maria. "Bandage her hands. We're going to discuss the next steps. For all of us."

~

The first phone call went to Mr. Willis. Walker rehearsed what she would say. How she would say it. Greg Willis answered. "Walker. Good to hear from you. I trust you all got home last night with no issues?"

Walker kept her voice calm and even. "The team was delayed when a dump truck lost its load in front of them. But no damage to the bus."

Greg laughed. "That's a relief. Your team could use a break."

Walker tapped her foot against the floor. He couldn't see her, so he couldn't read the nervous tic. "We could, sir. But we didn't get it. On the way home, we saw a fire at the Maugham house. We stopped to put it out. Our actions caught the attention of Police Chief Perkins. He made it clear he did not want me anywhere other than with my team. I can't teach tomorrow." *Or any day.*

Silence. "He what?"

"Made it clear if I was seen anywhere in town, I would be arrested for trespassing."

Silence again. "He said what?"

Walker looked up at Ron. She smiled without mirth. "I will give you his exact words, sir." Walker pulled out Jun's phone. Walker's voice held more tension than she liked. Pain will do that to you. "Ben conveniently called Jun while the conversation with Chief Perkins went on. Jun recorded the call as it came in. All very legal." She played back the recording. After it finished, she asked, "Were you able to hear the discussion?"

Greg fell silent. Finally, he spoke. "I heard it. All of it. I am sorry, Walker. I can tell you the sentiments you heard from the chief do not reflect the whole town. Probably not even part of the town."

Walker heard him sigh. She pressed ahead. "I haven't called Ms. Douglas yet, but I will once we are finished. I am sorry, Mr. Willis. I have thoroughly enjoyed working with the students." She dropped the formal speech, adding, "It almost makes me want to switch majors to teaching."

Greg's voice moved away from the phone. He must be talking to Patricia. After a few moments, he came back. "Don't quit on us yet. I have an idea. It may get me fired, but I think it's worth a try. Let me talk to Ms. Douglas, then I'll call you back. Will you do that?"

Walker closed her eyes. "Yes, Mr. Willis. I'll wait for you to call back. Thank you." She disconnected the call and stared at Ron, Maria, and the others. "Now we wait."

Ron shook his head. "Now we pray."

The group gathered into a circle, each person putting their hands on the other's shoulders. Walker joined as well. She suppressed the urge to shudder. *Friends. These are friends. No one here wants to harm you. We're praying, that's all. Praying. You can do this.*

Walker bowed her head. *Lord, I'm sorry. I've screwed this up. I know I have. Everything I do comes to nothing. I want to please You, but I can't seem to do anything right. Please, work this in spite of me. Glorify Your Name, with or without me. You don't need me. Don't let me interfere with what You are doing, especially with this team. My life doesn't matter. Your glory does. Please, Father.*

Ron began "popcorn prayer," each person saying one thing they were grateful for or praying for. They didn't go around the circle, but each person spoke as they felt in their heart. Walker stayed silent. *You know, God. You know.*

The group finished praying before the phone rang. Walker answered it. "Yes, sir?"

Greg Willis' voice sounded pleased. "Ms. Douglas and I have it figured out. Patricia will pick you up in the morning, as always. You're going to have an escort, however. Channel Seven News will be doing a ride-along. They're going to interview you about the rescue of Alissa and her baby. They never got their story. Tomorrow morning seems like a good time to do it."

Walker chilled. "No pictures. No recordings of my voice. Only print."

"Why no pictures? Would they put you in danger?"

Walker kicked at the floor, looked at Ron, looked at Maria, then drew in a deep breath. "One picture. Only one. Yes. It might." She shrugged to the side. "It might not. He may not care anymore."

"Who is he?" Greg's voice came across as gentle.

"A man named Robert Winger." She hesitated. "My biological father."

"Are you hiding from him?" Still gentle.

Walker dropped her eyes. "It's complicated. Yes and no." She stopped. "Mostly no. But yes."

Greg laughed. "You made that clear as mud."

Walker grinned. "Yeah, I did, didn't I? Okay, yes, I don't want him to know I'm in Indiana. No, I'm not hiding from him." She raised her eyes. "If he wants to come after me, he will." She caught Ron's gaze. "If the Lord wants him to come after me, he'll find me."

Greg paused. "I'll tell them only one picture. With only print media."

"Thank you. It will make it easier." *So, I can concentrate on dodging only one person at a time.* She thought a moment. "What happens during the day? They can't stay all day, can they?"

"They have been invited to observe your teaching methods. They want to see the new girls' basketball team you're setting up. It's wonderful local color."

Walker dropped her eyes. "Why are you doing this?"

"Because this town is better than Chief Perkins is making us out to be. We don't want anyone going away with a bad impression."

"Just civic pride?" She barely managed to keep the incredulity from her voice.

"Maybe. Maybe it's time someone stood up to the Police Chief." Greg's voice became firm. Stressed but firm. "And that's all I'm going to say about that."

Walker nodded, caught herself, and added, "Okay. I'll see Mrs. Willis in the morning."

Walker disconnected the call, then glanced up at Ron. "Right? Wrong? Indifferent?"

Ron smiled. "Right."

"But what about you? Or the team? Do you think the chief or anyone else will come after you because of me?" Walker sank down in her seat.

Ron held a hand out. "May I?" Walker nodded. He put his hand on her shoulder. "If the Lord is for us, who can be against us?"

"Lots of people. See what they did to the apostles."

Ron smiled. "See what the apostles did to the world. We're all here to be used by Him. Whatever He wants, we'll do."

Walker barely whispered, "But is this Him or me getting you into trouble?"

Ron sat on the cot beside her. "Walker, do you believe God is in control of everything?"

She looked up. "I'm trying to." She shook her head. "The only God I knew was my father. Fourteen years he controlled everything I said and did and thought. I now know the Only True God is in Heaven. I've given my life to Him." She bit at her lips. "But I don't know enough about Him to know what He will or won't do. I don't know what He wants from me or how to do it. I don't know what's His part or what's my part in all this."

Walker dropped her head. "Brother Matt says it's a learning process. I have to learn it as I go along. Faith." She dropped her shoulders. "I'm a slow learner." She nudged the floor. "I have too much to unlearn first, I think."

"It's not a magic formula. We all have to learn it as we go along." He smiled. "I'm still learning. If we're breathing, we're learning."

Jun grinned at them. "Ben learns deeper than most of us. His snoring at night must give him an advantage."

Ben tossed a pillow at Jun. Jun ducked, threw one back. Ron yelled, "No pillow fights!"

Three people launched pillows at him, burying him under linens and foam. Walker stayed out of the line of fire. Much as she wanted to play, she didn't need to risk further injuring her hands.

She could manage the pain. She could not let others see the burns bothered her. But at night would be another matter. It would be a long time 'til morning. Walker slipped from the meeting and went to her cot.

Maria waited for her. The med-major held a glass of water with two caplets in her hand. She motioned for Walker to take them. "These are for pain. I know you can ignore it. But it will make me feel better. So humor me."

Walker took the pills awkwardly, swallowed them, chased them with the water, then put her arms around Maria. She hugged the woman. "Thank you."

Maria grinned. "Thank you. Now I can sleep knowing I did my duty." She kissed Walker on the side of her head.

Voices screamed. Walker stood still, frozen. *No! No!*

You are loved. You are safe. You are protected. You are loved.

Memories tore at her.

You are loved. You are safe. You are protected.

Walker opened her eyes. Maria peered sideways at her. "Are you okay, Walker?"

She swallowed hard. "Yeah. I'm…good." She hugged Maria, then kissed her on the side of her head. "Thank you."

"Good night, Walker. If you need me, you know where my cot is."

Walker grinned. "Right next to mine. I'll find you." She slipped under the blankets, closed her eyes. Her body shuddered. She gathered it under control, sighed, and slept.

THURSDAY

Thursday morning. Walker showered early. Maria gave her a pair of vinyl gloves to keep her hands dry. *Yes, ma'am.* Breakfast was a repeat of the day before. Patricia Willis pulled in at seven to gather Walker. She had two passengers in the back seat. Walker squared her shoulders. Maria smiled at her. "You can do this. We will be praying for you all day."

Walker nodded. "I don't want the team to suffer because of me."

"We'll be fine. You take care of Walker. We'll see you tonight." Maria gave Walker a quick hug, then shoved her lightly to the waiting car.

Walker put one determined foot in front of the other. She walked to the car. She dug up her best smile and opened the front door. "Am I up here, or do we get cozy in the back?"

Patricia laughed. "No, you ride up here." She motioned to the man on the left. "This is Franklin Combs. He's the man who will do the interviewing." Patricia nodded to the other gentleman. "This is Bill Rankin. He's the photographer. He wants to video the girls playing ball. Ms. Douglas will deal with all the parental permissions and releases."

Walker shook hands with both men, then climbed into the car. She glanced at Patricia. "You have no idea how much I appreciate this. Or how much I would understand if you didn't want to go through with it."

Patricia pointed the car down the road. "Greg and I had a long talk last night before we decided." She looked in the rearview mirror at her passengers. "This is not for distribution."

The men nodded. Franklin stuck his fingers in his ears. "La la la." He took them out, smiling, "Understood."

Patricia continued. "Greg's been antsy. More than antsy. He's been nervous about things at the office for months. Whenever I ask, he tells me it's work, and he has to be the one to figure it out. But when you called last night, he seemed to snap. I still don't know what it's all about, but I got my husband back. He had a fire in his eyes. I saw a determination I haven't seen in a long time." She smiled. "So, I owe you."

Walker shook her head. "No. No, you don't. I haven't done anything except cause trouble. It's my most proficient skill."

Patricia laughed, then stopped. She eyed Walker. "You don't believe that, do you?"

Walker shrugged. She half-turned so she could see Franklin better. "What questions do you have?"

Franklin pulled out a small recorder. "Let's start with your full name."

"Walker."

"No first name?"

Walker shook her head. "Not yet. I'm still working on one." She saw Patricia's eyes twinkle. Shared joke.

Franklin raised his eyebrows but didn't pursue the matter. "I know you're with the relief team from Oakton. Why did you come?"

"Collectively, or me personally?"

"Both." Franklin leaned forward to get the recorder closer to Walker.

"The team came as a favor to Pastor Mars. Brother Matt Golding, the pastor of our church, is friends with Pastor Mars. Brother Matt heard about the tornado, then about Pastor Mars' church being destroyed. Matt asked a group of us to use our spring break to come down and lend a hand with rebuilding, or clean-up, or whatever they most needed. Twenty-five of us volunteered, which is why we're here. We all came because Brother Matt asked."

"What were you doing on the street Saturday?"

"Maria, Bobby Eller, and I were checking out the houses with burn damage. We—"

"Why those houses?" Franklin's eyes narrowed fractionally. "Curiosity?"

Walker chewed on the inside of her cheek. "Chief Zachary asked us to check for signs of arson."

"Arson? Why? Why the three of you?"

Walker rolled her eyes in her mind. Never where anyone could see. "One structure we found had been damaged due to arson. Chief Zachary asked me to inspect any other house which had been burned."

"You recognize arson? How?" Franklin plied his trade as an interviewer well. He managed not to sound incredulous.

"I have a varied skill set. Chief Zachary trusted my observations. He asked me to do a preliminary examination. Our team lead assigned Maria to accompany me so I wouldn't be alone. Bobby came with us to lend a hand if needed."

"Bobby Eller was part of the men's college varsity basketball team, correct?"

"Yes. Five of the men's team came to assist in the relief efforts. Bobby wanted to follow us, so he did." Walker studied the reporter's eyes. Did he share Chief Perkins' disdain? Did he blame her, too?

Bill Rankin snorted. "Was on the team. I heard he got booted, finally. No loss to anyone."

Franklin nodded but didn't comment. "So, you were examining the houses for arson. Is that what made you look at Alissa's house?"

Walker went through the finding and rescuing of Alissa and her baby. She finished the tale as they pulled into the school parking lot.

Walker pointed. "I've got company." She stared hard. Her whole being went on alert.

A police cruiser sat in the circle drop-off area of the school.

Waiting.

Franklin eyed the vehicle. "Officer Friendly, maybe?" The drug prevention program that brought police to the campuses of schools to reinforce the idea the police were the good guys.

Patricia shook her head. "The program was suspended six months ago. Chief Perkins said we didn't need it anymore. Students knew the good guys from the bad guys. He thought it a waste of money."

Franklin glanced over at Bill. "We're taking her in. Local news segment. The new girls' league. We want to see how they're taught. What they know. Let's go."

The two newsmen slid out of the car. Franklin opened Walker's door. "Between us. We're marching in, and we're not stopping."

Walker gave a single nod. Her nerves steeled. No show, no tell. Controlled. Give the enemy nothing.

Patricia called, "I'll hang out here to report what happens. From an objective observer, right?" She smiled, but her lips were a straight line.

The newsmen and Walker approached the teacher's entrance to the building. The police officer exited his cruiser. He marched toward them with a determined step. Franklin called out, "Morning, Officer."

The man rested his hand on his gun. He stared hard at Walker. "Are you the one they call Walker?"

Walker nodded. "I am."

"I have a warrant for your arrest." He stepped forward.

Franklin raised his eyebrows. "What's the charge?"

Before anyone could move further, Ms. Douglas and a well-dressed woman came out of the door. The woman had blonde hair, wore gold bracelets, and had a severe expression in her eye. She stalked up to the officer. "Yes, what are the charges? Let me see the warrant."

The officer glared at the woman. "You're not part of this."

She laughed. "Oh, yes, I am. I'm Leann Harlow, the legal

counsel for Ms. Walker. I want to see the warrant."

The officer went back to his patrol car. He got on his radio and called the station. "I'm here at the school to arrest Walker. A lawyer wants to see the warrant. She also wants to know what the charges are."

"Chief Perkins ordered her brought in on trespassing charges."

The patrolman walked back. "Trespassing."

Ms. Harlow raised her eyebrows. "Trespassing where? She's here on public property at the behest of an authorized school official. Her action does not constitute a trespass. You have no grounds to arrest her."

The officer sighed. "The chief said to bring her in. Those are my orders." He glared at the woman. "I'm going to follow orders."

Ms. Harlow smiled. "Of course, you are. But legal orders. What you have is not a lawful order. If you hinder Ms. Walker in any manner, she will be within her rights to sue this city for unlawful arrest and detainment. I don't know a judge who would support the chief on this. If you don't want to be dragged into court, I suggest you step aside and let Ms. Walker go about her business." Her eyes narrowed. "Understand?"

The officer scowled. He glared from Walker to Ms. Harlow back to Walker. "Fine. I'll tell the chief he needs to talk to you. He'll love being brought out here to execute a warrant."

Ms. Harlow offered a straight-lipped smile. "If he had one, he could. But he doesn't. Have a nice day, Officer."

The man slid into his patrol car and left. Ms. Harlow turned to Walker and extended her hand. "Pleasure to meet you, Ms. Walker." She handed Walker a card. "Put my number in your phone. Use it. I'll be on call 24/7 if anyone tries to give you any trouble."

Walker relaxed her muscles. "Thank you. I appreciate your help. I don't have money to pay—"

Ms. Douglas interrupted her. "Don't worry about it. It's taken care of. You come in and teach your students. They're waiting."

Franklin, Bill, and Walker walked into the building. Walker led the way to the gym where her first class warmed up, shooting baskets. Walker called them in. "This is Mr. Combs and Mr. Rankin. They are going to observe and film our classes. They want to see what we're doing to create our basketball league."

The girls all reacted with awe and the giddiness of young teens. But Walker put them through their paces. Period One, Period Two, Period Three…all the same. Franklin and Bill left for lunch. Walker suggested they return at three p.m. when the actual team practices and scrimmages were held. If they genuinely wanted a story.

They assured her they did. They would be back when school ended. Walker waved them off. She decided to go to Ms. Douglas' office. She knocked on the always-closed door.

"Come in, Walker." Walker opened the door and entered the windowless room. Ms. Douglas had chosen the smallest space to set up shop. Maybe the severe surroundings were for intimidation purposes. No one wanted to be called to the "inner sanctum." No one.

Walker took a seat across from the principal. "Thank you for intervening this morning. I'm not sure I'm worth all the trouble."

Ms. Douglas raised her eyebrows. "No? I think what you're doing here has tremendous value. Anything we can use to increase the self-confidence of my students is welcome. We're here to teach them they can succeed. Success in one area will wash over to other areas. If I can use basketball to keep the girls interested in school, it will be worth every ball they launch."

Walker smiled. Her whole body smiled. "I love your attitude."

"You didn't come here to tell me you love my attitude. What do you need, Walker?" Ms. Douglas leaned forward, folding her hands on her desk.

"I sent the men out until after school. Told them to come back and watch the real practice." Walker stilled her hands. "I'd like you to come see them work, too. I know we're going to do the competition on Saturday for the whole school, but I'd like you to see how far they've come."

Ms. Douglas rested her chin in her hand. "I'll see what my schedule is like." She grinned. "As long as I'm not fighting with the police chief over one of my teachers, I don't see why I can't be there."

Walker swallowed the grin. "Thank you, Ms. Douglas. I look forward to you coming."

The principal waved her hand, flicking Walker away. "Go do something constructive, girl. Practice your free throws."

Walker nodded. "Always. Free points. Can't afford to let those go." Walker turned and fairly skipped back to the gym. The rest of her day would glow. She knew it.

~

The final three periods went by. Period by period. Class by class. Walker refused to keep staring at the clock or anticipate the practice after school. Focus on the now. Be totally present where and when you are. Serve where you're placed.

Only after the final bell rang did she allow a sense of anticipation and excitement to grow. She ordered it, of course. Subjugated it to her will, to her control. Adrenalin served her, not the other way around.

The teams came in to begin their shoot-around. Franklin Combs and Bill Rankin returned. The men took up places on the bleachers. Walker immersed her attention on the court. Moving the ball became the focus. The goal. The single-minded purpose behind all they did.

The girls ran. They passed. They shifted. In, out. Dribble. Run. Shoot. Pass. Block. Two points. Over and over, side to side. The world blurred around her. All that mattered were the players. Only the game existed for her.

Until someone called, "Time!" Walker came out of her trance and stared around. She glanced at the clock. Six. The session ended. The girls sat on the floor or the bleachers, worn out and happy. Faces turned to Ms. Douglas. Expectancy. Hope. Desire. Walker saw it all.

Ms. Douglas smiled. "Now that is what I call basketball. I am proud of all of you. You did good out there."

The girls began cheering. Someone started chanting, "Walker! Walker!"

She checked around, startled and confused. *What did I do? What do they want?*

Carly ran up to her. The girl pulled her out on the court. "Ms. Douglas, you have to watch her. I mean, really watch her." She moved to shove a ball in Walker's hands, then stopped. Carly gaped with horror at the bandages. She looked up into Walker's eyes. "You can't play, can you?"

Walker took the ball. "I'll try. For you guys, I'll try."

No pain. Control the pain. Control the focus. You're trained for this. All those years? The only thing that matters is what you do. You're nothing. You have no value, no worth, unless you're pouring yourself out. Give it all. Nothing less than perfection matters. Do it. Do it.

Walker began dribbling the ball slowly. Small bounces. The voices in her head jeered her. Taunted her. Drove her. She moved out onto the floor, tentatively bouncing the ball faster and faster.

A part of her consciousness registered Ms. Douglas call out, "Enough. Stop." But the rest of her only heard the condemnation. The disapproval. The criticism. The continual attacks. Nothing was good enough. She wasn't good enough. She never would be.

Walker moved faster and faster. The ball became a blur in her hands. She whirled. She ran. She shot and spun and twisted until someone forcibly caught hold of her, stopping her. Walker came back to herself standing in the middle of the court. Ms. Douglas had hold of her. Arms around her, hugging her. Murmuring, "It's okay, girl. It's okay. Come back. You're here."

Walker stared up at her, trying to force comprehension or understanding. Ms. Douglas nodded her head. "Welcome back."

Walker glanced around the room. Her players were all seated on the bleachers staring at her in something near fear. Some were in tears. Walker lowered her head. Saw her hands. Blood stained the bandages bright red. Walker closed her eyes. *Be ashamed. Be very ashamed. Showing off. As if it will win you praise. You're a failure. You're nothing. You're—*

Walker moved over to sit on the floor in front of her players. Carly's eyes drilled into Walker's. Walker lifted her head. She sucked in her lips, turned her head off to the side. "I grew up never enough. No matter what I did, it wasn't good enough. Never. Ever." She gazed around at the team. "Like some of you who are fighting to be good enough. The voices in your head say you're too fat, too thin, too stupid, too smart. You'll never be anything or anyone." Walker sucked in a long breath. "If you don't change the script, it'll drive you to do things you'll never live down. Or with."

She laid her hands on her crossed legs, palms up. Ducked her head at the girls. "You all did something great here tonight. You put together a team. You girls played your hearts out. You're going to do it again Saturday in front of the whole school. Maybe in front of your parents and friends. You're ball players. You've succeeded in something people dream about."

She glanced from face to face. "But don't let it define you. What you do is not who you are. Who you are is here." She hit her chest with her fist. "It's what's inside you. It's who's inside you." Walker stared at the floor. "I'm not allowed to talk to you about the One Who saved me. But I'll tell you this. Four years ago, I got dumped on the streets of Oakton. Hard place. Drugs. Pimps. Thieves. Cutthroats. Homeless people walking around talking to the demons in their heads."

Walker stared at the blood on her hands. "I did what all street people do. I learned what I needed to stay alive. I had one thing driving me. Hate. I hated the man who left me on the street. Swore vengeance on him every day. Lived for one thing: to one day dance on his grave." She looked up at the girls. "Imagine as bad as it gets. That's what I had to do to stay alive."

She paused. Paused. Paused. "Two years in, someone told me

about a soup kitchen giving free food. No strings attached. Hot meals. A place to take a real shower, not run through city sprinklers." Walker shrugged. "Or a carwash if you're really fast. No. A place run by a man named Brother Matt Golding. He had two rules. No, three rules. No drugs, no fights. And no condemnation."

Walker sucked in her lower lip. "Two years I stayed there. Two years I watched a man live nothing but love and acceptance. Two years I listened to him talk about peace and joy and light and life."

She leaned forward. "I learned I needed what he had. Who he had. I couldn't go on living on hate. I had to give it up. So I did."

She smiled slightly. "This is the part I can't tell you about because we're at school, and I'm a teacher. But you can talk to me later if you want to know, or if you really can't figure Who I'm talking about." She lifted her head. "But it's not magic. It's not instant. I'm not perfect. I'm a mess. I'm still the woman with the voice in my head telling me everything I'm not. Sometimes he wins. Sometimes I win." She gazed at her hands. "This wasn't one of those times. But you deserved to know what drives me."

Walker stared at the floor again. "Be the best you can be. Be everything you're meant to be. But be it for the right reasons." She lifted her head to meet the girls' eyes. "Not because someone else is driving you. But because you are. Go after what makes you you. Go after it hard. Never, ever stop. But do it because it's who you are inside." She smiled at the girls. "Now go home before your parents think I've kidnapped you." She stood. "I'll see you tomorrow. Good night."

The girls slowly dispersed, moving in twos and threes, talking in hushed tones. Walker moved to Ms. Douglas. She met the principal's gaze. "I apologize. I lost it." She drew in a deep breath. "Will you forgive me? Then fix my hands?"

Ms. Douglas put an arm around Walker's shoulders. "Come on, Walker." They walked down the hall. Ms. Douglas' eyes smiled. "I'd say you won. Those girls will never forget what they saw and heard tonight."

Walker stopped. "What about Mr. Combs and Mr. Rankin? I missed them. Were they still there?"

Ms. Douglas moved Walker on down the hall. "Yes, they were there. I trust them to be men of discretion. Your story will be safe with them."

The principal took Walker to the first aid station. She unwrapped Walker's hands to examine the burns. She peered aghast. "Walker! You need to go to the ER for this."

Walker shook her head. "No. No ER. No doctors. Not here." Ms. Douglas stared at her, her eyes narrowing. Walker lowered her eyes. "I don't want to go through all the litany of things wrong with me. Every time I see a different doctor, they want to call children's services, or the local police, or some other form of law enforcement. I have to tell them the entire story of my life. In the meantime, they don't fix what's wrong because there are too many other problems. So please, bandage my hands. I promise you I'll see the doctor at the clinic in Oakton when we get back. He knows me." She chuckled. "He's given up on me, but he does know me."

Ms. Douglas sprayed Walker's hands with antiseptic, lathered them with burn gel, then wrapped them with clean bandages. She shook her head when she finished. "I don't know about you, Walker. Sometimes, I just don't know."

Walker smiled. "That makes two of us, Ms. Douglas."

Together they walked to the waiting team bus. For the first time, Walker and the team arrived back at camp in a timely fashion. Walker shook her head. Sometimes miracles happen. Maybe tonight was one of them.

FRIDAY

Friday morning, Patricia arrived to pick Walker up. No chaperone. No police presence. No police threat. Walker climbed in and looked around. "You think we're in the clear today?"

Patricia nodded. "I'd say so. Ms. Harlow talked with Chief Perkins. She assures me he won't be issuing any more summons for you. She's made him rescind the ones he put out as well. You're cleared to teach today with no interruptions." She grinned slightly. "Whether you can make it through the day is another story."

Walker chuckled. "Yeah, well, I'm going to do my best. A plain, boring day would be wonderful. Regular classes, then practice again. Tomorrow, the girls have their exhibition. It should be illuminating for some in this community." Walker scanned the road ahead. Just in case. Constant vigilance.

Patricia agreed. "Girl sports attracting as much attention as the boys? That'll stretch the imagination of more than a few people. But it's time we moved from the fifties to the current decade."

Walker glanced at the driver. "Will you and Coach Willis be there?"

Patricia turned a corner, stopped at a school crossing, then motored on down the road. "We wouldn't miss it. We're both invested in what you've done at this school. We're proud of you."

Walker lowered her head. "Be proud of the girls. They're the ones who did the work."

"But you showed them how. Take some pride in your

achievement, Walker." Patricia eyed her quickly before focusing on the road again.

Walker shook her head. "I'm just a tool the Lord uses. He does all the work. He could have used anyone. Lots of people out there He could have used. He got stuck with me instead."

Patricia pulled the car to the side of the street and stopped. She stared at Walker. "The Lord isn't 'stuck' with anyone, Walker. He didn't choose to use you because He couldn't find anyone better. He chose you because He knew you were the right person for the job." She studied Walker a moment. "You don't believe me, do you?"

Walker shook her head. "I'm nothing, Mrs. Willis. The Apostle Paul talked about being the 'chiefest of sinners.' Well, I think I took the title from him. God uses me as an example of what not to be. I'm okay with it. At least I can serve some purpose."

Patricia scowled at her. "Walker…I wish you had two names because I'd throw them both at you. That's the most inane thing I've ever heard you say. It's also an insult to God. He chose you because He loves you. You're not some second-class, second-choice creation. He loves you as a father loves his child."

Walker stared at her hands. Her fingers were crooked from being broken over and over. Those were the wounds she could see. She controlled her voice, but it still came out small. "My father hated me. From the moment I was born, he hated me." She looked up, met Patricia's eyes. "He told me so. Every time he had opportunity, he reminded me what a disappointment, what a total disaster I was. I destroyed his life. Stole his future. He promised he would return the favor in my life."

Walker turned to stare out the window. "I accept the Lord loves the world. I accept He died for all the ways I fall short. I accept He chooses to use me." She faced Patricia. "But love me? Maybe for what I can become. But not for who I am. Never for who I am."

Patricia's voice became soft. "You told the girls to go after what's inside. What's inside you, Walker?"

Walker remained silent for several moments. Patricia put the car back in motion. She smiled gently. "I think you and your Creator need to sit and figure it out. Because I think His opinion of you is very different than yours is."

Walker nodded. She gazed out the window. "Mrs. Willis, would you mind stopping at the Maugham house? I have to check it out. The longer it goes without someone inspecting it, the more chance there will be for evidence to be tampered with or destroyed."

"You don't think the other night's fire could have been an accident?"

"No, I don't. I believe someone set it to hide what happened the night of the tornado." She glanced at Patricia. "Please? I won't be long. There are only a couple things I need to inspect. You can wait in the car."

Patricia turned the car toward the cul-de-sac. "No, I won't. I may be a trophy wife, but I can still be useful." She smiled a tight-lipped smile. "Let's do this."

~

Mrs. Willis pulled the car around the back of the house away from sight of the road. Walker climbed out. She waited as Patricia stuffed her purse under the seat. The woman joined Walker at the back door. Walker untucked the bottom of her shirt to use to open it. Leave no DNA to confuse the issue. They walked inside, heading straight to the kitchen.

The ceiling on the single-story home had been burned away. Charred roof rafters stood naked over their heads. Walls leaned blackened with smoke and ash. Wallpaper peeled from around the windows. Scorched lumber lay across the sink. The linoleum floor had bubbled and melted in sections.

Patricia paled. Walker laid her hand on the woman's arm. "Are you sure you don't want to wait in the car?"

Mrs. Willis lifted her head. "No. I want to see what you see."

Walker stepped through the sagging doorframe into the dining room. She passed through the semi-standing family room into the hallway to the main bedroom. The door had been closed, still in its frame, but burned from floor to ceiling. Walker took a deep breath, used her shirt again, and opened the door.

One look proved enough. The marks on the mattress told her all she needed to know. She gingerly pulled her phone from her pocket with two fingers. She handed it to Patricia. "Can you take pictures of the bed?" She held Patricia's eyes, then repeated, "Can you?"

Patricia nodded. She raised the phone and snapped several shots. Her eyes filled with tears as she worked. She choked. "They died in their sleep, didn't they? Right here in their beds."

Walker nodded. She didn't answer beyond the nod. No need.

They walked to the two smaller bedrooms. Patricia photographed the same evidence. The children died as their parents did. In their sleep. Never feeling a thing. *If there is a consolation, I guess that's it.*

Walker closed the doors, leaving them as they'd been found. She stared at the floor. Patricia shook her head. "Why didn't they hear the sirens? Why didn't they wake up?"

Walker lifted her head. "They were dead before the storm hit. Someone murdered them, then tried to cover it up with the fire." She motioned toward the back of the house. "I need to check the furnace. I think they died of carbon monoxide poisoning." She led the way to the utility room off the kitchen but didn't find the furnace. "It must be in the garage."

Patricia nodded. "They usually are in these homes. Keeps you from hearing them come on and off all the time."

Walker opened the garage door. The space had been totally consumed in the fire. Walls were barely standing. The ceiling had caved in. Debris covered a blue SUV parked against the side. Children's toys lay melted on the floor. Carbonized remains of a bicycle hung from the studs still standing. The floor had blackened from the heat.

Except for one spot. Walker motioned to Patricia. "Pictures, please. There."

Mrs. Willis snapped several images. "What does it mean?"

Walker closed her eyes. "It's where the arsonist died. His body protected the floor from scorching."

Patricia turned away, lowered her head, gagged. Walker touched her arm. "I'm sorry. I'm so sorry. I didn't want you to see this."

Patricia raised her head. Determination burned in her eyes. "No. If this is how we bring a killer to justice, I needed to see it." She caught Walker's eyes. "You shouldn't see this alone, either."

Walker nodded. "Better to have two witnesses. You're someone whose word they'll trust. I'm still an outsider here." She moved to where she could see the controls on the furnace. Her speculation about the gas proved correct. The safety on the pilot light had been hammered, making it useless. The thermostat sat on high. Gas pumped into the home while the family slept. The wonder was the place hadn't exploded when the fire had been set.

The tornado. Walker nodded. The tornado sucked the gas out before the fire. Or enough of the gas to keep it from knocking down half the houses in the neighborhood. Patricia snapped pictures without being prompted. Walker waited until she finished. "We should leave."

Mrs. Willis handed Walker the phone. Walker waved her off. "Do you know how to upload pictures to the cloud?"

"I'm pretty tech-savvy. I can do it." Patricia tapped in the necessary commands. Walker suggested, "Send them to your husband. Also, to Ms. Douglas." She stopped, added, "Send them to Ron. His number is in my phone. Warn them all. They might not want to open them. But I want copies sent to as many people as possible."

Patricia glanced up. "Why?"

"So, the evidence can't be lost or destroyed. Someone might think if they destroy my phone, the proof disappears. I want the proof kept safe in multiple places."

Patricia worked to comply. "Do you always think of the dark

side, Walker?"

"Most of my life has been lived on the dark side. So yeah, my natural self goes there." She ducked her head to the side. "I want to think people are honest. To think maybe they are good. But that's not the world I come from." She smiled at Patricia. "I'm learning a different reality, though. One person at a time. Like you."

Patricia finished relaying the pictures and the messages. "Thank you. I do try." She motioned. "Let's get out of here."

They left the same way they'd come in, leaving as little evidence of their presence as they could. Patricia climbed into the driver's seat, started the car, then declared, "Now we go to the police."

Walker's eyes flared. "What? No. We can't. Not after Chief Perkins tried to have me arrested and deported. I don't trust him."

Patricia pulled the car onto the street. "We have to trust someone, Walker. The whole police force can't be crooked. I won't believe that for a moment." She held Walker's gaze. "I may be naïve. But I have to believe there are still honest people." She nodded to herself. "I'll prove it to you. You'll see."

Walker stilled the screaming inside. *Bad. Bad. This is all wrong. This is not going to end well for either of us. Lord, please, help us. Protect Patricia, anyhow. Do with me as You will, but protect her.* Walker stared out the front window. She marshaled her inner strengths. Whatever happened, she would not go down without a fight.

~

Walker texted Ms. Douglas to let her know she would be late. And where she and Patricia were headed. In case she didn't make it back. Never can be too careful.

Patricia and Walker entered the police station. They stopped at the front desk. Mrs. Willis smiled. "Officer Talbot. Nice to see you. How are the twins doing?"

The young patrolman at the podium returned her smile. "Mrs.

Willis. They're doing fine. Mimi says JR rolled over. Sissy won't be far behind. How can I help you?"

Patricia's face drew down into a frown. "Walker and I have information about the Maugham family murders. We need to talk to whoever is in charge of the investigation."

A deep voice boomed from around a corner. "Is that Patricia Willis?"

Walker cringed on the inside. Never on the outside. Never show weakness or surprise.

Chief Perkins walked out into the lobby. "Well, well. Walker. Didn't think I'd see you here. Especially without your lawyer. Is she hanging around outside?"

Walker kept her tone even. "I didn't think I needed a lawyer to present evidence of murder, Chief Perkins."

"What evidence? What murder? No one murdered I know of."

Patricia stepped forward. "We went through the Maugham house as Chief Zachary requested."

Before she could continue, Chief Perkins cut her off. "Ah ha. Chief Zachary. Wants to be in charge of everything, doesn't he? Who is he to suggest an investigation? What would he know about murder?"

Patricia's eyes darkened. "Chief Zachary is responsible for investigating all fires, Chief Perkins. You know very well. The fire at the Maugham house…"

Again, he cut her off. "Yes, I know. Very suspicious. So he thinks. Isn't that why he appointed Ms. Walker the junior fire marshal, hmm? Did he give her a badge, too?" Perkins laughed. Walker noted Talbot chuckled. But she detected an edge in the younger officer's tone. Uncomfortable. Good. Patricia might be right.

Perkins waved at the two women. "Come in my office. I want to see this evidence." He stopped. "Oh, wait. If you went in there without authorization, you contaminated the scene. Now we'll never be able to prosecute anyone. Very nice. Did Zachary think of that possibility?"

Patricia lifted her head. "We didn't touch anything. We left no evidence of being there beyond our footprints. Those can be eliminated from suspicion."

"Can they now?" Perkins motioned for Walker and Mrs. Willis to enter his office. He smiled as they passed him.

The room served as the control hub for the station. Three computer monitors sat on a table against one wall. A large mahogany desk centered on the other. Whiteboards with the day's roster filled one wall. Corkboards with maps stretched out over another.

Hard-backed wooden chairs sat opposite the desk. Chief Perkins sat in his rolling desk chair. The kind which leaned back for comfort. For show. Walker and Patricia took the hard chairs. Patricia repeated her statement. "Yes, the footprints can be eliminated. You will have our shoes to compare the prints to. A good office can make that determination."

Perkins drawled. "A good office, hmm? Meaning if we can't tell your shoeprints from someone else's because you walked over the evidence, we're not a good office?"

Walker caught Perkins' eyes. "There were no other footprints, Chief Perkins. No one has been in the house since the rescue crews took out the bodies."

"You know because? Oh, I forgot. You're the junior fire marshal. You've had years of training to be able to detect that. Forgive me for assuming my thirty years of experience and four years of schooling could match your two years of big-city education."

Nothing the chief said would bait Walker. She nodded. "You're forgiven. If you don't want the pictures we collected, we'll take them to the press. I'm sure they would appreciate something for the front page."

His eyes narrowed. "With your face on it? That should go over well in this community. Your reputation could use some polishing."

Patricia looked from Walker to the chief. "What are you talking about? Walker's reputation here is nothing but wonderful. She saved Alissa and her baby."

Perkins snorted. "All by herself. Isn't that how the story went? Didn't have any help from her friends, did she? I understood Bobby was there, too. No one gave him any credit for his part in it, did they? No, it was all about Ms. No-first-name Walker here. Why don't you have a first name, lady?"

"I haven't picked one out yet. I'll let the paper know when I do." Walker sat back in her chair. Calm. Collected. Nothing would phase her.

"Picked one? So, you're not even using your real name?"

"Walker is my real name. The Department of Records in Oakton says so."

Perkins glared at her. "You think you can waltz in this town and stir things up to suit you? Let me tell you something, missy. I know what you are. So do the parents of this town. Your hero days are over."

Patricia stood up. "We're done here. You don't want our evidence. We'll take it to the paper like Walker said." She jerked her head sideways. "Come on, Walker. We're leaving."

Perkins smiled. "Sit down, Mrs. Willis."

Patricia glared at him. "You can't tell me…"

"Your husband is an employee of this town. If he wants to keep his job, I suggest you sit." He leaned back in his chair, resting against the wall. "I have the ear of the city council. We can hire or fire without cause. Don't give me cause."

Patricia froze. She stared at him, her face confused and in shock. "You're threatening my husband's job?"

Perkins smiled. "I think you misunderstood my meaning. I would never threaten." He let the sentence hang. When Patricia's eyes registered understanding, he said, "I asked you to sit down. You say you have evidence of a crime. I'd like to see it." He held out his hand. "Give it to me."

Walker pulled out the phone with two fingers. "I'll send you the files."

"You'll hand me the device. How do I know you won't tamper with them? Photoshop has the tremendous ability to establish someone's guilt where there is none." He smiled at Walker. "I'm sure you know what I'm talking about. There might be pictures on here of you some evil person could take. Who knows how they could alter them to make you appear like you were doing all manner of illicit activities."

Walker smiled back. "Not from my phone. I don't take those kinds of pictures."

He continued to smile. "Someone else might."

Walker handed the phone to the chief. "The Lord will defend my honor, Chief Perkins."

"I'm sure the good people of Rallins will be thrilled to hear you think so. But I wouldn't count on his support. Not from what I hear about you. Street rat? Street tramp, more like it."

Walker shrugged. "The passcode is 5555. I'll want it back when you've pulled the files."

Perkins shoved the phone into his desk. "Yes, well, when my technicians can get to it, they will. Until that time, I'll hold it here. For evidence. Chain of custody. I'm sure you understand."

Walker held his eyes. "I understand completely, Chief Perkins."

He smiled. "I'm happy you do." He looked over at Patricia. "Since you've delivered the evidence, you can leave. I'll be certain Walker gets transported where she needs to go."

Patricia shook her head. "I don't think so. I brought her in, and I'll take her back with me."

Perkins shook his head. "You really don't understand, do you, Mrs. Willis? Your husband is a good man. I've enjoyed working with him these past few years. But I find if I can't work with the wife of one of the city employees, I can't work with the husband, either. If you leave now, your husband Greg and I will have many more happy years working together. But if you continue to be a problem, I'll have to recommend to the city council he be terminated."

Walker stood. She held Patricia's eyes, narrowing her own. "Go on. I'll be fine. Go home. Call a friend, go out for coffee. Everything here will be okay."

Patricia searched Walker's eyes. Walker smiled. She reached up, hugged Mrs. Willis, then whispered, "Call Greg. Leave town. Tell Ron to do the same."

She pushed back, still smiling. "Thanks for everything. I'll see you tomorrow, I'm sure."

Patricia smiled. Her eyes reflected relief. "You're right, Walker. Everything will be fine. The Lord has this." She turned to Perkins. "Will I see you at the exhibition on Saturday?"

"Exhibition? Girls playing basketball?" He scoffed. "I don't think so. I like a real game. Men only."

Patricia didn't argue. She took one final look at Walker, then exited the office. Walker heard her call, "I'll see you later, Talbot. Tell your wife I said hi. I'll be over with some brownies this weekend. Promise."

Walker didn't hear the man's response. She returned to sitting opposite the chief. "You'll take me to the school? I'm still teaching."

"No, you're not. Ms. Douglas should be finding out the school superintendent has suspended her for hiring an unlicensed instructor with a shady past. Too bad. Ms. Douglas could have retired in June. But now, no one's going to hire her again. She has you to thank for that. Don't you love all the trouble you've caused people?"

Walker smiled at him, her lips in a straight line. "It's something I'm good at. Among other things."

"Yes, well, I'm certain whatever those other things are won't help you much. You can sit here until I'm ready to transport you where you need to be."

Perkins rose. The chief exited his office, stomping down the hall. Walker waited a few moments, then got up. She walked into the back of the station where the patrol would be working. Walker sallied down the corridor, peering into the offices as she went by. She made eye contact with as many patrol persons as possible, smiling and waving. *Let them see me. Make sure they know I am here. Who I leave with. They can't all be under his thumb.*

A patrol woman in her mid-thirties glanced up. She caught Walker's eye. Walker gave her a wide, innocent smile. "Hi! Officer..." Walker read her name off the plate on the woman's chest. "Officer Kirk. Can you do me a favor?"

The woman cocked her head. "Yes, young woman. Can I help you?"

Walker pled her case quickly. "Chief Perkins is taking me back to my people. I'm not under arrest or anything, so would you mind being my chaperone? I'm really not comfortable riding with a man alone." Walker grinned. "Even a man in uniform. Since I'm not under arrest or anything." She repeated herself to be perfectly clear about the matter.

Before Officer Kirk could answer, another voice called, "I'll do it."

A brunette woman in a dark pantsuit pushed a desk drawer in, stood, and stepped in front of Walker. "I'm not doing anything important. I'll be happy to ride along with you wherever the chief takes you."

Walker smiled. "Would you? Thank you..."

"Detective Anson. You are?"

"Walker." Before the detective could ask, Walker added, "Just Walker."

Anson nodded. "Okay. Walker. I'll ride along with you."

Chief Perkins stomped into the area. "Walker, I told you to wait in my office."

Detective Anson waved him down. "She's fine. She came out to find an escort."

Chief Perkins growled. "It's not necessary. She'll be safe with me. I've escorted more than a few drunks to their place of residence.

She's no different."

Walker smiled. "But I'm not drunk. Or stoned. Or in any way incapacitated. I could easily call for a ride home."

Perkins' eyes hardened. "You do that. You call your people to come get you. But tell them to take care. The roads can be hazardous. Accidents happen all the time."

Walker returned his stare. He would not threaten her or her people. Not while she drew breath.

Anson stepped between them. "It's no trouble, Chief. I've got my stuff gathered. I'll follow you out to the cruiser."

Perkins glanced at Anson. "I said it's not necessary, Detective."

She smiled at him. "And I said I'd ride along. Station protocol dictates that if a female requests another female be present, she must be accorded the courtesy. We wouldn't want to run afoul of the law, would we?"

Perkins smiled. "Why of course not. We always follow the law, don't we? Walker and I will meet you outside." He pushed Walker forward.

Anson returned his smile. "I'm right behind you, boss."

Perkins stalked behind Walker, a glowering presence over her shoulder. He swung around her to get the door leading to the parking lot. The chief opened the back door to a patrol car. "In."

Walker slid in. Before Perkins could close the door, Anson slid in beside her. "Now we can be chauffeured wherever you need to go."

Walker dropped her eyes as Perkins moved around to climb in the driver's seat. "Thank you. This could get ugly."

Anson's eyes twinkled. "Try being a woman in this station. I'm accustomed to ugly." She winked at Walker, then reached for a coin-sized device in her pocket. She shifted it to Walker's hightop while smiling at the chief's back. "We women have to look out for each other." She mouthed, "Microphone tracker."

Walker nodded. Perkins settled in the front. Anson pulled out her phone. "I'll text the kid I'm going to be a little late. He'll have to start lunch without me." She punched in some numbers, then dipped her head to Walker. "All done. Everything set."

Perkins glared in the rearview mirror but put the car in motion. He turned the car off the main street and headed out of town.

Walker closed her eyes. Memories of a million scenarios flashed in her mind. Successful escapes. Failed attempts. Impossible situations she'd navigated before. Others that ended in disaster, captivity, or worse. Her head pounded again. Too much thinking.

What did the Lord want her to do now? She'd revealed the crime. Was that His only purpose for her? Did she matter anymore? Would He cast her aside to whatever fate the chief had in mind?

See? God is no different. Use you, then discard you.

I will not leave you or forsake you.

Sure seems like it from this side of the locked doors.

Walker cleared her mind. No anticipation. Only readiness.

They drove over roads Walker hadn't seen before. She committed the directions to memory. In case she had to find her way back. If she lived to find her way back.

Anson made light conversation. "You must live way out in the sticks. I don't think I've ever been out in this neck of the woods."

Walker nodded. "Me, either."

Perkins didn't comment. He focused on driving. Further and further into the empty countryside.

As they neared a stand of trees, Anson asked, "What did she do to you, Chief? Expose one of your cronies?" The detective's eyes narrowed, her voice hardened.

Perkins snorted. "A little late to ask now, isn't it, Detective? She thought she'd get an ally to help her escape. Instead, she gets a partner in death. I kill you both. That way, I get rid of two problems at the same time."

Anson shrugged. "Had to happen sooner or later. You weren't going to let me keep digging into your affairs. But I'm not the only one who's been poking around, you know."

Perkins shook his head. "Nice try. My boys are loyal to me.

They wouldn't ever cross me."

Anson raised her eyebrows. "Who do you think arranged my transfer here? And why?" She chuckled. "You've got trouble coming like you've never seen before."

"I'd better get out of Dodge, hadn't I?" Perkins drove the car to the side of the road. Walker could see a steep embankment but not what lay at the bottom of the hill. Perkins pulled his service revolver. He pointed it at Walker. He ordered, "Get out of the car, Detective."

"Can't. Doors only open from the outside. You don't want to get blood all over your unit. Way too incriminating. It never comes off, either. You can't even burn it to make it disappear."

Walker eyed the detective. Did she have another meaning? A different reference?

Perkins rolled out of the driver's position. He crossed in front of the car and came at the passenger side door. Anson whispered, "Get ready."

No, no, no. They never stand behind the door. You can't kick it open and knock them over. They always make you get out by...

Perkins stood in front of the door as he opened it, slinging it wide. Anson smiled at him. "Thank you, Chief." She crawled out of the car to stand beside him.

He motioned. "Put the gun on the ground. Slowly or Walker dies."

Detective Anson pulled her weapon from her shoulder holster. She laid it on the ground at his feet. Perkins picked it up, his gun still trained on Walker.

Walker shimmied out behind Anson. The sound of splashing water reached her mind. A river. Everything in her screamed, *NO!*

Memories she had buried swarmed up from the depths to terrify and paralyze her. Rivers meant death. Fear clamped around her being. Compressed the breath from her lungs. Wrenched her from the present to a past she'd suppressed for so many years. All of it came flooding back.

Anson's voice in her ear reached for her. "Walker? Are you

okay?"

Screaming. Falling. Gagging. Screaming. Gagging. Screaming...

Gunshots. *Run!* More shots. Cursing.

A needle jabbed her. *Poison?*

No. Too easy to find in an autopsy.

What? Narcotics?

Does it matter? There's a drug flooding through our system.

She had to gain control. Had to slow her heart rate. The slower her heart pumped, the slower the drug would act. She couldn't fight two battles at once. Perkins knocked her down. Her body flipped over. Over and over. Down the embankment to the river.

The river. The river. She didn't have the strength to fight. She couldn't do it. She would fail. He would win. He always won.

I am with you. Always. Call to Me. I am here. I will answer.

Walker landed on the rocks. The water splashed her face. Terror seized her. He was there. Smiling. Gloating. Reveling in her defeat.

I am with you. Always.

Help me! Help me! I don't want to die. I have to beat him. I have to. I can't let him win.

Not by power. Not by might. By My Spirit.

Agony filled her. The drug blazed in her system. Burned in her mind. Seared her being. Again. *Lord, give me strength. I need Your power to beat this. Please.*

Time meant nothing. Did it pass? Did it exist? Reality melded with hallucination. Monsters became men, men became monsters. Her mother died and rose again. Only to die again. And again. And again. Her brother—A-One—lived and died a thousand times before her eyes. People from the streets extended a hand up. Slapped her down. Kissed her. Kicked her.

Cackling wove through the nightmare. *"You're worthless. A blight on creation. You should never have been born. You soil everything you touch and kill anyone who tries to love you. Die. Do the world a favor. Die."*

She whispered, her voice broken, "I don't want to die."
Live.
"I…don't have…the strength."
Not by power. By My Spirit.
She cried out in confusion, "What Spirit?"

She stood before the Lord. Enthroned in glory. High and lifted up. King of Kings. Lord of Lords. Creator of Heaven and Earth. She groveled at His throne. "Help me."

The King stepped from His throne. He gathered her in His arms. Hugged her. Held her.

Walker cried out, "Save me, please."

"For what?" He asked, His voice gentle.

"I can't let him win. I can't. I have to live." She moaned on His shoulder.

"Revenge can't save you. Only The Spirit can save you."

She cried from the depths of her anguish, "What Spirit? How do I overcome?"

"In forgiving. Give away your anger. Your desire for revenge. Your hatred. It kills you more surely than the drug in your veins."

Walker screamed, "He hurt me!" Her spirit shattered into a million shards. She sobbed. "He hurt me. I loved him, but he hurt me."

The arms around her held her tight. They were warm. Safe. Loving. "I know, child. I will repay. Not you. Not your job. Mine. You have other work."

"What work? I lived for revenge. What else is there?"

"Love. Forgiveness. Peace. Joy. Experience it. Spread it to others."

Walker stilled in His arms. She sniffled. "I don't know how."

He kissed her. "Learn."

The vision faded. The taunting voices returned. The insults. The slurs, the derision. Tearing at her being. Trying to pull her down.

And yet…

Yet in her soul, a peace. An untouchable light Who could not be extinguished. She recognized it…Him. He'd been there all along. Her hate drowned His Voice. She could drown Him out again. Could hold the anger, bitterness with both hands. Clutch it tight to her chest as her lifeline.

But then she would die.

Or she could let it all go. Reach out to Him with empty hands and take His yoke and live.

Did she really have a choice? Walker whispered, "I'm sorry. Teach me to forgive him. To forgive him like You forgive me. I want to learn. I want to live."

Fire still burned in her veins. She shivered. She convulsed. She wretched. She curled into a ball and moaned. Her head swam. The world pitched and swung and rolled. Time flew. Time froze. Consciousness came and went. And came again.

Walker lay in the dirt and mud, water lapping over her arm. She rolled to her side, groaning with the effort. Her head protested, sending lightning strikes of pain through her brain. She silenced it. She may have forgiven, but it didn't negate all her training. She would master her body.

Walker sat up an inch at a time. She shuddered, shivered, trembled. She closed her eyes. "Help me, Father. Your way or no way. What do I do now?"

Waves of nausea pulsed through her. Walker lay back on the rocks. She let her head swim on its own. After an indeterminable time, she heard a car pull up and stop. Walker clawed the tracker from her shoe. Buried it in her fist. She slowed her heart rate. Slowed her breathing. Everything she'd been forced to learn as a child, she did. "Play dead." One of the skills she'd perfected out of self-defense.

Heavy boot steps crunched down the side of the hill. She recognized the scent. Recognized the sound of the breathing. Chief Perkins. Come to see if she had truly died?

He kneeled beside her. Turned her head to the side. Felt for a pulse. Walker slowed her heart to a near stop. She could hold it down for eight, ten seconds. Longer than an average person would check for a pulse. Chief Perkins proved to be no exception. He stood. Then he caught hold of her arm and leg. He rolled her into the river, out into the water where the current would carry her downstream.

Walker maintained her death pose. *No panic. You are not alone. You are safe. You are loved. Do not freak. Keep the tracker out of the water.*

When she could hold her breath no longer, she rolled over, gasping for air. She had floated well clear of the road, out of the line of sight of the chief or anyone else. But she had no strength to climb out of the water. She floated along, bumping lightly into tree limbs, twirling around in a small eddy, then finally lapped ashore on the river stones. She could only lie there. "Father, it's all up to You. It always has been. Whatever You want, Lord."

Convulsions wracked Walker's body. Walker groaned. She clenched her teeth. "I will not yield. I will not yield." Her breath came in short gasps. She closed her mind. She would not break. Walker fought the drug's effects. She would not yield. It would not consume her. She moaned. Her world became all-consuming anguish. Nothing reached her. Nothing penetrated the roaring of blood in her ears, the thundering in her brain.

Brother Golding's voice filtered through the noise. He read words of hope. "The Lord is a strong tower. Run to Him and be safe." "He will be with you in the fire and flood. The fire will not consume you. The flood will not overcome you." "Nothing can separate you from His love."

Words of life. Walker grabbed at the lifelines in her mind. She recalled the Lord's words, *"Not by power or might, but by My Spirit."* She clung to them like the drowning woman she was. She whispered, "Help me, please. Help me." Time meant nothing. It jumbled together again. She lost all sense of reality. If time passed, she didn't know it. Now existed, nothing more.

Until eventually, the tremors, the seizures slowed, then stopped. Her breathing leveled off. The blood ceased pounding in her ears.

Incrementally, she regained control of her body. She opened her eyes. Nothing registered. She couldn't focus.

Voices seeped into her consciousness. Not close, but not far away, either. Calm, rational voices. Unable to stand, Walker inched along the riverbank to get closer. Maybe friend? Maybe foe? Only one way to find out.

She stopped edging when she could hear the voices clearly. Chief Perkins and Detective Anson seemed to be having a discussion. Perkins' voice sounded irate. "You should be dead. Now I'll have to kill you over again."

"Sorry to mess up your plans, Chief. How will you explain the discrepancy in the time of death?"

"Why should you care?"

"I want to hear how your mind works. How you think you'll get away with six, no, seven murders. I don't think even your overmasters will excuse that many deaths. It looks incompetent."

"What overmasters?"

Anson's voice became surprised. "You mean you arranged all this yourself? Forgive me for underestimating you. I thought for sure you had help."

"That's right. Big city detectives can't conceive us plain folks can come up with an idea on our own. Have to have someone more intelligent show us." Perkins radiated disgust.

"Skimming money off construction doesn't take an advanced degree. Covering it up takes some skill. Or an accomplice. Like in the controller's office?"

Perkins laughed harshly. "No, I will not sit here and detail how I did everything. You'll have to solve this mystery on the other side of death."

Walker could hear the shrug in Anson's tone. "Oh, I figured it out. I even have friends on the inside who are pulling the records now. You'll be picked up and carted off as soon as you show your face in town."

"Sure you do. Who?"

"I guess you'll have to solve that mystery on the other side of death yourself."

Walker shivered. Where were Anson's friends? The ones at the other end of the tracker? Shouldn't they be here by now? Were they coming? She inched closer. She saw Anson sitting on the riverbank with Perkins looming over her. Walker picked up a substantial rock. Did she have the strength to throw it? Which way? *Lord, You felled Goliath with a stone. Launch this.* Walker threw the stone as far and hard as she could. It plopped harmlessly in the water midstream.

Perkins swung around and fired at the noise. Anson launched into him, caught him around the middle, and drove him to the ground. Walker grabbed a thick branch, used it to climb to her feet. When the combatants rolled over, Walker smacked Perkins in the head. It stung him. He caught her eyes and froze. "You're dead!"

Anson took the split-second of inattention to grab Perkins' gun, roll away from him, and point the weapon at his middle. "Freeze."

Perkins moved. Anson fired a shot, hitting within an inch of his feet. Perkins froze. Anson leaned against the rise in weariness. She smiled at Walker. "Good of you to show up. I thought you were dead, too."

Walker shivered. "Born again. You ought to try it." She sank to the ground out of reach of Perkins.

Anson shook her head. "Cute. Real cute." She motioned to Walker's feet. "Tracker stay dry?"

"Not in there. I held it all night. They should be able to find us."

Perkins' head swiveled around. "Who?"

Anson smiled at him. "My backup. Who may be slow, but they will be here." She motioned for Perkins to sit a safe distance away from her and Walker. The detective asked Walker, "How are you? What happened up there?"

Walker hung her head. "I'm sorry. I froze. The river…"

Anson shook her head. "Don't apologize. If you had tried to save me, the chief would have killed you, then me. If I had tried to save you, the timing would have been the opposite, but the outcome the same." She eyed Walker up and down. "What did he do to you?"

"Shot me up with something. Narcotics. Most of them are out of my system." She shuddered. "Not all. Most."

Anson's voice became soft. "I'm sorry. You don't know how to build a fire, do you?"

"All but the ignition part."

"We'll skip it."

Perkins stared hard at Walker. "How are you alive? I checked. You were dead."

Walker smiled, her lips pulled tight across her face. "I have a varied skill set." *Which I never thanked You for. Ron was right. You do use it all. Even the "useless" lessons. I'm sorry for complaining.*

Tires crunched over gravel on the road above the ravine. Perkins and Anson exchanged glances. Anson tipped her head to the side. "Want to take a bet whose people those are?"

Perkins sneered, "No."

Anson nodded. "Must be mine."

Car doors slammed. Voices yelled, "Eve!" "Detective Anson!"

She called back, "Down here, lads. Bring some warm coats or blankets. We're freezing."

Shoes slid down the side of the ravine. Three bodies followed the shoes. One body looked familiar. Walker's mouth hung open. "Mr. Willis?"

Greg Willis took one glance at her, wrapped his arms around her, crowed, "You're alive! I was so afraid…"

Walker buried her head in his shoulder. Anson warned, "She still could be if you don't get her to a hospital."

The word "hospital" surged life back into Walker. She jerked her head up. "No. No hospitals. No doctors. I don't want…"

Anson glared at her. "You want him convicted?" She jerked her head toward Perkins. Walker glanced from the detective to the police chief and back again. She nodded. Anson continued, "Good. Then shut up. Go to the hospital like you're told. Let the doctors document your wounds. Let them take blood samples. Evidence. We want to put him away for a very long time."

Walker swallowed hard. "Yes, ma'am."

The three newcomers helped Walker and Anson up the hill, then into the car. A second batch of police arrived to take custody of Chief Perkins. Walker saw him be led up the side of the gully, be handcuffed, and stuffed in the back of a police cruiser. Walker leaned her head against the backseat. Anson put her arms around her. "Warmer this way."

Walker nodded. "Yes, it is." Greg covered them with a coat, turned the heat on high, and peeled out across the gravel. Walker closed her eyes. *Thank You, Lord. Now all that's left is the girls' exhibition. Thank You for bringing me back before it happens so I can coach them one final time.* She let her mind drift, shut it down, and slept.

~

Walker sensed she was wrapped in a blanket in someone's arms. Light poured in through a window and warmed her face. She lifted her head to soak it in.

A voice—Patricia? Ms. Douglas?—called, "Walker? Are you in there?"

"Yes." Did they hear her? Did she have enough volume? Did she care?

"We're here with you. You're not alone. We've got you. You're safe." Patricia. Her arms held Walker.

Walker forced her eyes to focus, to identify the who, what, where of her situation. She recognized Ms. Douglas' front room. Walker lay on a couch, bundled under blankets. Patricia sat beside Walker, cradling her head and chest, holding her close against the tremors and seizures. "How long?"

Patricia smiled. "It's Saturday afternoon. You've been in and out since Friday evening."

Ms. Douglas appeared in Walker's line of vision. "How are you doing, Walker?"

Walker nodded her head, unsure of her ability to say anything. Saturday. What happened to Friday??

Walker sat up slightly. "Detective Anson?"

"She's fine. She has a squad of people cleaning up the police department. Chief Perkins is under arrest for kidnapping, attempted murder, murder, and maybe a few other associated charges we can throw at him. Chief Zachary has gone through the Maugham house. He found everything the way you said it would be." Ms. Douglas added, "The fifth person in the house died of a gunshot wound." Ms. Douglas' face hardened. "Your arsonist." The principal sat in a chair opposite Walker. "They can't directly tie him to the arson at the church, but the authorities seem to be leaning toward rolling the two together."

Walker bowed her head. *No one is asking my opinion. I'm not giving it.* But there were still questions. "Why? What did they do to Chief Perkins?"

"Drew Maugham reviewed the orders coming in for the new police complex. Some of the figures didn't look right. He contacted Greg Willis. Greg reviewed them, then spoke to Chief Perkins. Perkins threatened him to keep quiet about the matter."

Patricia added, "He battled about it for weeks. He knew the right thing to do. But Chief Perkins has a heavy hand around here. Greg didn't know what he would do in retaliation. But my husband finally contacted someone at the county level. That's where Detective Anson came in. She transferred here to investigate. Drew wasn't satisfied with the investigation. He thought she was moving too slowly. So, he confronted Chief Perkins. Chief had the Maughams killed, shot the arsonist, then thought he'd gotten away with it all. Once you came, he had to figure out some way to silence you as well. The rest, you know."

It explained how she got to where she was. But people were missing. Where were Ron and Maria? The team? She lifted her head again. "My team?"

"They're working the tear-down at Pastor Mars' church. Once

Chief Zach identified the fifth man as an arsonist, the demolition could begin." Ms. Douglas smiled. "You can't believe how happy your people are to finally be doing what you came for."

Walker nodded. "I'm sure."

Patricia gave Walker a gentle hug. "You're not still in the hospital because Ron said you would recover better in a home. He says you have a serious aversion to hospitals. Once the police had the evidence they needed, the medical staff let us bring you here."

"Ron's right." Coming off drugs in the shelter of someone's arms rather than a sterile environment made it easier. At least for her. No telling what her rescuers went through. Walker sat up, trying her strength against the sluggishness of her muscles. She would master them. She would…

Walker sighed. "Can you help me sit up, please?"

Patricia smiled. "Certainly." She maneuvered Walker to a semi-upright position. Walker waited for her equilibrium to settle, then turned to Patricia. "Thank you." She held the woman's eyes. "Thank you."

Patricia laid her head against Walker's. "You're welcome, young woman. I'm glad you're alive and recovering."

Ms. Douglas sniffed. "I'll be glad when I get my living room back." Her eyes twinkled.

Walker drew in a deep breath. "Yes, ma'am. I will vacate the premises as soon as possible." She stretched the muscles her brain could contact. Some responded. Others protested. Walker forced her legs to move off the couch and touch the floor. Both legs informed her there would be no standing any time soon, thank you very much. If she wanted to face-plant on the floor, they would be happy to oblige. Beyond that, she was on her own.

"What time is it?"

"It's about four. Why?" Patricia cocked her head.

Walker relaxed her shoulder muscles. "Are the girls practicing for tonight? Is the exhibition still on schedule?"

Ms. Douglas and Patricia exchanged glances over Walker's

head. Walker's gut tightened. Ms. Douglas nodded. "Yes, the girls are practicing. Greg is supervising the gym while May runs them through their paces. They're exceptionally excited for this opportunity to show what you've taught them."

"I didn't teach them anything except work hard." Walker stared at the floor. If she forced the issue, she could stand up. Maybe she could still catch part of the practice. Walker ignored the sniggering in the back of her mind. She dictated to her body, not the other way around. She tensed the muscles in her legs. Walker gathered whatever reserves she had and leaned forward.

Ms. Douglas stood and put a hand on Walker's shoulder. "Relax, young woman. You're not going anywhere. You're not strong enough. You can argue all you want, but you are staying put for another night. We moved the exhibition to Monday night as it is."

Walker leaned back in defeat. "If I promise not to coach, will you let me go watch?"

The exchange of looks for the second time heightened Walker's tension. She studied Ms. Douglas' eyes. "What's wrong? Tell me."

Ms. Douglas sat down. Patricia put an arm around Walker's shoulders. Walker closed her eyes. "What is it?"

Ms. Douglas' voice became soft. "The girls were impressed and moved by your testimony. It made a lasting impact on them." The principal smiled. "Yes, there were questions off campus." She lost her smile. "But some of the parents weren't as impressed. They…had some…objections…to you teaching the class. A group of them banded together to approach the superintendent."

Walker lifted her head. "Chief Perkins made comments about me teaching. I thought he made it all up." Life drained from her. "They don't want me to teach?"

"No, Walker. They don't want you to teach any classes. You're not licensed, so the superintendent agreed with the parents. You won't be teaching anymore."

I am with you. You are a new creation. You are My beloved. As far as the east is from the west, so far have I removed your past from you.

Walker swallowed. "I won't be coaching, either. Right?"

Ms. Douglas nodded. "Right."

Walker closed her eyes. Drew in a deep breath. "They don't want me around the girls. Right?" She opened her eyes and watched Ms. Douglas.

"I'm sorry, Walker. I am."

Walker glanced from Mrs. Willis to Ms. Douglas. "They didn't suspend you, did they? Take away your retirement? They can't."

"No. The superintendent refused to go that far." Ms. Douglas' eyes burned. "Some of the parents wanted him to. But he told them they'd have a revolt on their hands if they did. The entire teaching staff would quit."

"Good." Walker nodded. "I'm glad some of them have some sense."

Ms. Douglas smiled. Alligator smile. "Right. I resigned."

Walker shot forward. Her brain objected. She slid back. "You didn't."

"I did."

"You can't. Those kids need you. They need someone who will listen to them. Someone they can talk to and know you understand. Or will try, anyhow. You can't quit."

Mrs. Willis smiled. "The superintendent didn't accept her resignation. He told her she needs to take the weekend to think about it. We told her the same."

Ms. Douglas shook her head. "Won't make a difference. My mind is made up."

Walker dropped her head to the side. "Please. Think about it. My life could have been different if I'd had you as a teacher. Or a principal. Or just someone who'd hear me. You can't quit."

Ms. Douglas patted Walker on the shoulder. "I'll think about it. For you. Now, you need to get some more rest, young woman."

Walker leaned back on the couch. She chewed the inside of her mouth, then dipped her head. "I guess I'll try to sleep some more. Tomorrow I can rejoin the relief team." She shrugged. "Hitting walls with a sledgehammer may feel good."

Patricia smiled. "Maybe I'll join you." She shifted off the couch so Walker could stretch out. Walker lay down, curled around the pillow, and closed her eyes. Patricia patted her shoulder. "Sleep. I'm glad you're doing better. Tomorrow will be better still. 'Night."

Walker nodded. It would have been a good time for tears. If she knew how to cry.

MONDAY

Sunday the team rested. Pastor Mars held a simple service on the grounds where the church would be rebuilt. The team had a day of rest. Muscles were rested, bruises allowed to heal, and everyone generally relaxed. Monday, they went back at it hard.

Ron gave Walker strict orders to do nothing more than watch, soak up the sunshine, and be an encouragement to her teammates by breathing. She managed to obey all parts of her assignment for the first hour. And the second.

By the third, sitting in the sunshine became boring. Being an encouragement by breathing came easily. But watching while others worked became a vexation to Walker's soul. She slid off her perch on the picnic table and struggled up the hill to join the workers.

Ron narrowed his eyes, pointed to her, yelled, "Back to your table, wench!"

Walker shook her head. "Nay, kind sir. A boon, please. Let me carry water to those who thirst."

Ron dropped his theatrics. "Walker, you…" He stopped. "Why do I bother? Yes, you can carry water. But only one bottle at a time. I don't want a relapse."

Walker shuddered. "I don't, either. Believe me. I'm not going to challenge anything. Honest. I just want to be helpful." She glanced side-eyed to make sure Maria didn't hear her. She'd deliberately chosen the term 'helpful' not 'useful.' No rebukes. Not today.

You are loved. You are My chosen vessel. I chose you before you were born.

Walker distributed the water bottles to the sweatiest workers. She won smiles, "thanks," and "good to see you alive" comments. She could almost allow herself to believe them. Almost.

You thought your past was gone, right? Underneath the blood of the Savior? What a joke. No one ever forgets. A new creation? Not in this life. Maybe not even in the next one. You will forever be the loser you are.

If being a Christ-follower didn't make her "good enough" to work with girls, why go to college? Why all the work, the study, the volunteering when she would be rejected in the end?

Walker curled up cross-legged on the ground. She bowed her head. She didn't deserve…

Maria's voice startled her. "Stop. Stop it right now."

Walker lifted her head. "Stop what?"

"Overanalyzing everything. Blaming yourself. Thinking this is all your fault, your punishment for past failures, or however you're taking responsibility for the attitudes of others."

Walker tipped her head. "Doing what?"

Maria sat beside her. "Listen, I know you're hurt. I hurt for you. I hurt with you. It's not the first time we've been called out for what we were in the past." She held Walker's eyes. "You know my story."

Walker nodded. She tapped fists with her friend. Maria looked at the ground. "I'm still at Brother Matt's mission because my parents don't want me at home. They're afraid of my influence on my little brothers and sisters." She held Walker's gaze. "So I know. I do. It's hard, it hurts, and it's reality. We know who we are in the Lord. Other people don't see it. All we can do is live it every chance we get."

Walker sucked in her lower lip. "I wanted to see them play. See them get the accolades they deserve."

Maria stood up. "What time is the exhibition?"

"Six to seven."

Maria spun around. "Hey, Ron!"

Ron put his sledgehammer down. "What?"

"We're stopping at five. Get the team cleaned up. We're going to go watch Walker's girls play ball. All of us."

Ron walked over to the two women. He eyed Walker. "Are you sure you want to do this? You sure it won't make it worse, not being out there with them?"

Walker shook her head. "No. I want to see them. I want to see them being honored and cheered. I don't have to be on the floor. I don't have to be where anyone knows I'm there. All I want to do is see them."

Ron studied the ground a moment. Finally, he turned and yelled, "Quitting time is five." Several cheers rewarded the announcement. Ron continued, "Anyone who wants to come watch Walker's girls play their exhibition, be cleaned up and ready to go by five-thirty."

More cheers. Walker stood up and hugged Ron. "Thank you."

He eyed her sideways. "May I?"

She nodded. "Yes." Ron hugged her, then let her go. Quickly. Walker laughed.

~

The bus pulled up behind the school, away from the general parking. Ron suggested, "Let's slide in by twos and threes. I don't want to announce we're here. We don't need to give anyone a reason to make a scene. It would detract from what the girls are doing. Walk in, sit down, and keep it casual."

Jun laughed. "Yes, we will infiltrate the crowd."

Walker sat on her bench until twenty-four other students disembarked. Ron watched her a moment. "Are you coming? This is what you wanted."

Walker nodded. "I'll go in soon. You guys all get settled. That way, if anyone recognizes me and throws a fit, you can watch the game for me."

Ron opened his mouth, then stopped. He nodded. "I'd love to say you're wrong, but I can't. I'll see you inside."

Walker waited. And waited. And waited. She heard the crowd cheering. Listened to the teams being introduced. Coach Willis announced each player's name and position. Probably all according to script. No "the girls have worked hard" or "the inspiration for this game is" or any other preamble. Names and nothing else.

She whispered, "Let your play speak. Show 'em what you've got. Let it loose, ladies." Walker moved to the farthest door from the entrance. She slipped through the employee entrance. Snuck around to the back of the gym. Climbed the bleachers to the highest row. Sat as far away as she could be to still be in the same facility. No one would see her. No one would know she had come.

Walker lost herself in the play on the floor. The girls were spectacular. They played with energy. With style. With excellence. They made believers of skeptics. The passes were crisp, on target. The ball sailed up and down the court. No one dogged it. No one flagged. The players rotated in and out seamlessly. They performed like the well-oiled unit they were.

When the clock ran out, they huddled together, linked arms, and spread out in front of the crowd. Cheers and voices of approval, shock, and awe greeted them. The reception passed Walker's imagination. She whispered, "My girls. Well done."

Franklin Combs walked out on the floor to congratulate the girls. He handed each one a rose for their efforts. He asked them about their practices, their work, their dreams going forward. Each girl on the team had the chance to talk.

Carly waited until the end. She took the microphone from Mr. Combs. Her eyes narrowed as she looked over the building. She gazed over both sides of the bleachers. Trying to find someone. Someone in particular. Walker stiffened.

Carly waited until the room quieted. "I learned an invaluable lesson this weekend." She searched up in the stands. "I learned my Sunday school teacher lied to me."

Murmurs. "What's more, my pastor lied to me." Silence. "Worst of all, the Bible lies." She gazed around the room. "I've always been taught when we ask, Jesus forgives us. He makes us a new creature. 'Old things pass away, and all things become new.'" She turned around. "Isn't it what we're taught?" She laughed harshly. "All the bad we do is removed from us. Cast in the sea of forgetfulness. What a joke."

Walker heard the break in the young woman's voice. "I thought it was true until this week. We had a new teacher. A teacher with a past. But she loved Jesus. She loved Him so much she couldn't stop talking about Him. Even when maybe she shouldn't. But that's how much He meant to her. He saved her life, and she wanted the world to know it."

Carly took a step forward. "But her past didn't get forgiven. Or forgotten. No, her past is unforgivable. I began to wonder if hers is, maybe mine is, too. Maybe none of us are saved." She shrugged. "But that's what I learned." She handed the microphone back to Mr. Combs.

Walker slipped down from the bleachers, staying out of sight. She would catch Carly on the way out. Correct the misunderstandings. The girl had to know the difference. Didn't she?

Before she reached the bottom bleacher, a chant began. It started with one of the girls on the team. "Walker."

The team took up the refrain. "Walker. Walker."

Someone in the bleachers picked it up. "Walker. Walker. Walker." *If that's Jun, I'll kill him.*

Someone else stomped their foot to the syllables.

Not every voice joined the call. Some faces were positively hostile. But the majority picked up the mantra. "Walker. Walker. Walker."

Maria hissed in her ear. "Get out there. Go. Now." Walker turned and stared at her friend. Maria pointed to the center of the gym for emphasis.

Walker swallowed hard. She straightened her spine, lowered

her shoulders, stepped out onto the pine.

Cheers replaced the calls. The girls' team raced across to mob her, jumping up in their enthusiasm. "Did you see us?" "Did you watch?" "Did you see me score my goal?"

Walker let them wind down a notch, then waved them to silence. "Yes, I saw you. Yes, I watched every move you all made on the floor. I could not be more proud of any of you. You did fantastic. You were fantastic." She hugged each girl one at a time. The team set Walker in the center of their locked arms and faced the bleachers.

Cheers and applause echoed around the room. The girls made a choreographed bow. Then another. Then another. Finally, Mr. Combs stepped forward. He handed Walker the microphone. Walker waited until the room quieted. There remained a buzz of disapproval, but she ignored it. She glanced at the people in the stands. "These are your daughters and your sisters. They played their hearts out to show you they can. They can work hard. They can go after a goal. They can achieve it. They wanted you to see their passion. Not for basketball. For life. For all of it. They want you to know they aren't second-class anything. They deserve the same honor and respect any other athlete gets. Which includes the boys' college varsity since they're here, and I can pick on them."

She grinned at Virgil and Larl. Greg Willis pointed at her in jest. She pointed back. Walker lowered her head a moment. She looked up. "Carly—I know, she's May. But we have an agreement. I call her Carly, and she doesn't skip my class."

Carly grinned and hugged Walker. Walker hugged the girl back. "Carly had a lot to say about pasts and backgrounds. She's right. My past will follow me."

Watch what you say. Remember where you are. You can't talk about the Lord.

What are they going to do, fire me?

Walker continued, "Being forgiven by Christ won't change what I did. People who see me will judge me. I'll live with it because when my Savior sees me, He sees me the way I am in Him." She smiled at Carly. "The same way He will see you when you come to Him. You're beautiful and loved and chosen. No one will take that from you. Ever." She kissed Carly on the cheek and whispered, "I love you, Carly."

Carly's face dripped tears. She kissed Walker back. "I love you, too."

Walker motioned with her head. "Hit the showers, ladies. Then go home. Remember, you have school tomorrow." Together they walked off the floor.

TUESDAY

A large crowd of well-wishers (and some "good-riddance" wishers) came to see the relief team head back to Oakton. Pastor Mars thanked them for their work at the church and throughout town. Dinner on the grounds was served one last time. Walker made sure to dodge Cheryl and her youngsters. She'd say goodbye to them later. But she would eat in peace.

The hard goodbyes were the personal ones. Walker stepped up to Virgil.

He smiled at her. "You still owe me a game and a date with friends."

Walker shook her head. "Next time." She held his eyes. Reached out and hugged him. "Take care of yourself, Virgil."

He grinned at her. "I kept my arms!"

Walker shoved him lightly. "Go away." She hugged Larl as well. "Take care of your mom."

"Always."

Ms. Douglas stood beside her son. "You take care of you, young woman."

"You sure you want to retire? You're not going to reconsider?"

"Nope. I have life to live." Ms. Douglas smiled slyly. "Maybe I'll run for office. Chief of Police. What do you think?"

Walker laughed. "I think that would be fantastic. I'd vote for you if I was registered in this state."

She hugged the Willis's last. "Thank you for everything." She smiled at Greg. "I appreciate everything you did for me." She turned to Patricia. "Thank you for saving my life."

Patricia hugged her. "Oh, you're welcome, Walker. You promised you'd come back and see the town when it gets rebuilt."

"I will. And it's not Walker. It's Collin. Collin Walker."

Patricia grinned. "Why Collin?"

"Because you said you were tired of callin' me Walker. I think it has a nice ring to it."

If you enjoyed "Twisted," follow Collin Walker's further adventures with "Verdict at the River's Edge," Book One in the Collin Walker Series.

What terrifies you?

In the dark recess of your soul, what is it that you've managed to avoid, to hide, to bury deep, never to be faced? And what if the Lord asked you to face that fear for no other reason than, "Because I'm asking?" What would you do?

Welcome to Collin Walker's world.

Collin Walker, a social worker from the inner city of Oakton, Ohio comes to Camp Grace for what is billed as "an extreme sports camp." Her single purpose: to show her ward, Rob Sider, that there is more to life than the streets "...show you can be strong and still love, win without cheating, and succeed in life without all the bells and whistles..." Collin has no way of knowing that God has other plans for her week: facing a lifelong terror of rushing rivers, and perhaps her greatest fear of all, the possibility of real love.

Available now: Verdict at the River's Edge

Excerpt of Chapter One:

As soon as Collin Walker's feet hit the bottom step of the bus, she heard it. The low, pounding, distinctive rumble of a river. A river somewhere nearby. She froze, overwhelmed by the panicked impulse to fight her way back upstream through the departing campers, dive under the backbench seat and not come out until the week ended. A thought kept circling through her head: *Dear God in heaven, there's a river.*

A hand on her shoulder interrupted her mental breakdown. A voice dripped sarcasm. "Hey, caseworker lady. You getting off this bus or what? They's some of us what wants to visit the facilities, you know? Been a long trip. Move it."

Life returned to Collin's feet, and she stepped off the bus, moving aside to let the remainder of the forty odd campers—and their vastly odder counselors—disembark.

Odder? Is that even a word? Collin shut down the internal tormentors before they could continue. *Sane. I will be sane for the remainder of this trip. And you all will keep your comments to yourself.*

It might be easier to believe without the cursed cackling in her head.

Collin would deal with her demons later. She'd been dealing with them all her life. So what's another day? Collin leaned against the side of the bus to get her bearings and her breath. She wrapped her arms around her chest and began slow breathing to bring herself under the rigid control she learned over the years. In. Out. In. Out. In.

Rob Sider, her ward for the week, stepped in front of her. His eyes narrowed slightly in confusion. "Who you fightin' in there, huh?"

Collin jiggled her whole body to release the tension. "I'm working on a plan to beat your sorry anatomy in hoops."

Rob stepped back with half a grin. "No wonder you having a tough time of it."

Collin held a hand in front of his face. "Watch it, bro. You know the old saying, 'He who laughs last—'"

Rob interrupted "—didn't get the joke the first time. I ain't afraid of you or any plan you got." He crossed his arms over his chest.

Collin felt herself relaxing. She lay a hand on his shoulder. "What say you and me meet on the backcourt tonight about nine and see if this plan I got works?"

"Backcourt? What backcourt?"

Collin sighed. "Rob, if this place has more than one court, it has to have a backcourt. I'll meet you at nine on the backcourt, and we'll see if you're as good as your mouth on foreign soil."

Rob grinned evilly. "My mouth got nothing to do with it. Be my feet an' my hands do the talking. You ain't never beat me yet, and you ain't never gonna."

"Never's a long time, my friend."

Rob took two sliding steps back. "You'd be the one to know 'bout long times!" He took off running for the lodge.

Collin dropped her head, grinning all the while. Twenty-six made you old in Rob's world. Somedays, it felt old. She looked around the entrance to Camp Grace, forcing herself to suppress the ominous and omnipresent sound of the river. High in the mountains of West Virginia, planets away from the streets of Oakton, where she worked and lived and fought and died…

The sun lowered itself behind the towering trees, which sheltered the lodge. Even though the evening had barely begun, the valley would soon disappear in darkness. Vibrant green grass grew natural and wild in meadows and patches where the trees relented to allow sunshine. Flowering vines trailed up and around stumps, fence posts, and downspouts. Birds darted in and out of sight; fat crows cawed their superiority yet fled from kamikaze sparrows defending their territory. Paradise. At least for the week, if she could handle it.

For Rob, she would handle it. Collin cast off the shadows and moved slowly toward the entrance to the lodge. A "challenge camp," the flyer said, offering traditional and extreme sports to entice hardened and jaded youngsters ages ten to fourteen. Rob made the cut-off by four months. The camp presented as state-approved—but not sponsored—which meant the cost needed to be borne by the parents or the counselor.

Collin stopped at a "Welcome to Camp Grace" sign. She drew circles in the dirt with her foot as she looked at the map showing the "You Are Here" arrow.

The flyer stated financial aid or grants were available on request. But when Collin called the camp to request, the cost proved so ridiculously low she wondered if the camp could be real. She sent off the registration and fees to the address in West Virginia, only to have both returned. The registration approved; the fees waived.

Collin quit circling the dust and moved along the path. Quiet and careful inquiries to other attendees revealed they, too, were attending *gratis*. She determined then to find out all she could about this camp— who owned it and why they would be so interested in street kids. Paradise had its snakes, too.

Collin sharpened her focus and headed inside. She dodged a lone maintenance man unloading and carting the luggage. He may have smiled at her. He may have even spoken to her, but Collin didn't notice. Head down, eyes straight ahead. Focused. Something about this set-up read wrong, and she would be the one to find it. For Rob's sake.

I will not let anyone use these kids to fulfill some philanthropic need to make themselves look good. Not my kids. Collin marched through the lodge doors.

~

Collin followed an escort down the corridors to the female side of the building. She noted Rob's room number and the name of the counselor overseeing him.

The escort explained, "Only one child to a room unless they have requested otherwise." The escort smiled. "We know some of these children may be sleeping alone in a room for the first time."

Alone in a room? Some of these kids will be sleeping alone in a bed for the first time.

Collin envisioned a few sleepless nights for some of the younger campers. *They'll work it out.*

Luggage sat outside the doors, waiting to be carried into the rooms. Another guide brought two girls down the hall and presented them to her as her charges for the week, then left. Collin knew the girls well. Jill and Marites, both ten, roomed adjacent to Collin. They seemed the giggly, innocent type, not ones you would suspect of being in serious trouble. Certainly not on the verge of being placed in juvenile lockup. But Collin knew their jackets—and their counselors—well. Which explained why the girls were here and the counselors weren't.

A sign on the back of the door explained the basics. Collin read the salient features aloud. "Breakfast hours are seven to eight, no exceptions. Latecomers go hungry."

Jill tossed her head in disgust. "Can't make me go hungry. Gotta feed me, right? Anytime I want, right?"

Collin shook her head. "Nope. The card says healthy snacks of carrots, celery, apples, raisins, and assorted power foods are freely available at the health bar below the main concourse. Which means they have food available. If you like vegetables and fruit instead of pancakes and eggs."

Both girls gagged. Collin nodded. "I thought as much." She turned back to the sign. "It says lunch and dinner hours will depend on whatever the activity of the day is." She paused. "Which I'm sure they will explain later."

Jill and Marites looked at each other, then shrugged in unison. Collin mirrored their motion. "It goes on to say you should stow your gear and report back to the room just inside the doors where we came in at the head of the hall."

Fearing too many directives or instructions would be lost—or ignored— Collin said, "First things first: hand over the phones." Before the girls could deny the existence of said devices, Collin warned, "Having a phone will get you sent home at your parents' expense. I know you both have them. Give them up." Reluctantly the girls handed over the phones.

Collin checked her roster to make sure the numbers matched. Once verified, Collin said, "Go store your stuff and wait for me here. I'll be right out."

The girls closed the door. Collin shut her door and listened for a moment. Yep, still there. Even with the windows closed and black-out drapes reaching below the jams, she could hear the rumble of the bane of her dreams. *It doesn't matter. Sound can't hurt you.*

Who says you have to go any closer than the lodge? No one. Get over it.

Coward.

Collin escorted the girls to the main hall and looked for Rob. She found him sitting by the window, staring up at the heavens. Rob did not stop staring but acknowledged Collin's presence by whispering, "I never seen anything this big before. Never been anywhere this big." Outside, pine trees soared to vast heights. Towering canyon walls marched away out of view to either side, their craggy peaks barely visible to human eyes.

Collin sat down beside him. "Now, you get an idea of what awesome means."

Rob turned and looked at her for a moment. "I guess so." He looked back out the window. "Can we go out there?"

"My guess is the next order of business will be introductions, a list of rules to remember, question and answer sessions, and maybe dinner. Then free time and finally bed."

Rob gave her a curious look. "You been to these camps before?"

"A few." She motioned toward the crowd gathering in the center of the room. "Let's join the circle and see if I'm right."

Rob reluctantly followed Collin to where campers and counselors congregated. They joined in time to hear a man speaking. "If everyone could close in enough to hear and be heard, I would appreciate it."

The speaker waited as the crowd moved in closer. "Good. Welcome to Camp Grace. I am Steve Parks, camp director. I won't bore you with our history; if you're interested, we have literature at the office. If you're not, we'll save a few trees. Our mission is simple and is directly for you campers."

Collin eyed the man. *This is where it gets real. What do they really want?*

Most of the youngsters raised their heads, curious. Rob kept his eyes fixed on the floor, feigning non-interest. The director continued, "Our goal is to teach you one thing: you can."

A girl spoke up. "Can what?" General murmurs echoed the question.

"You can. Can do anything you set yourself to do."

An older boy snorted. "Yeah, right. Like I can jump like Michael Jordan."

Mr. Parks smiled. "Maybe. Have you tried?"

"Sure, man. I can't do it."

"Have you practiced the steps he takes? Have you exercised and worked out and jogged? Do you sweat like he does?"

The boy snorted again. "No."

"Then, you won't jump like he does." Mr. Parks looked around the room. "Doing isn't something magic. It's something you make happen using all the resources and talents and abilities you have."

Some heads nodded. Some dropped. Collin sensed they all listened, though.

Mr. Parks continued, "This week is to show you you can. We're going to give you opportunities to do and try things you've thought about, dreamed about, had nightmares about, or just wanted to see."

A nightmare or two flashed through Collin's mind. She shuddered. *Not now.*

"None of them will be simple. All will require thought, sweat, practice, and in some cases, teamwork. In the morning, we have a camp tour for anyone who can greet the daylight without a snarl. Snarlers can go in the afternoon." Laughs and catcalls followed, with elbows thrown for effect.

Mr. Parks glanced around the room at the campers. His eyes sparkled with what Collin took to be enjoyment. "You'll have the opportunity to sample some of our offerings this weekend, weather permitting. There is a partial list of activities on the board at the end of the hall to give you—I started to say 'fodder to chew on'"—the director chuckled—"but most of you would have no idea what I meant. So let's put it this way: it will give you something to think about."

He looked pointedly at the adults in the room. "A word to you, counselors." A grown-up head or two came to attention. "Show your kids you believe, too. Sign up with them. Show them it works."

As a means of closing, he said, "There are a few important people you will get to know. The first, we hope you never see: our camp physician, Dr. Wallace." A casual-looking gentleman in blue jeans, khaki shirt, knee-high cowboy boots, with sandy-blond shoulder-length hair pulled back in a ponytail, waved from his seat on the front desk.

Director Parks pointed to the side of the hall. "My assistant, Leeann Baker, will make any arrangements in case of emergencies either here or at home." An older woman, slightly overweight, wearing a red business dress, waved from her position against the wall. "Ted Johnson is our activities director."

Another wave from another strategically placed employee. Collin noted they seemed to be surrounding the group. Sizing up the kids? Watching group dynamics?

Mr. Parks continued, "Jeff Farrell staffs our maintenance crew." The director looked around then added, "And he appears to be missing." He looked at the activities director, who mouthed, "Generators." Mr. Parks nodded slightly.

The director finished with, "Our chief cook, Chef Michael, is downstairs preparing dinner. Enjoy your meal. Afterward, you may walk around outside or use the ball courts and recreation rooms. There is an indoor pool or you can sample the library. Relax and have fun. Enjoy your weekend, because come Monday, you're mine." He grinned evilly, rubbing his hands together. "Any questions?"

If there were no one felt inclined to offer them. "You may consider yourselves dismissed."

The crowd moved off toward the dining hall. Collin caught Rob's sleeve. She warned, "Remember we've got an appointment tonight. Don't eat too much."

As they rounded the corner to the cafeteria, Rob sneered, "Caseworker lady, I could eat everything they got and still beat you."

The size of the buffet staggered them both. Rob did a double-take. Collin's mouth dropped. Grilled chicken. Beef tips. Fish. Pasta. Hamburgers. Fries. Pizza. Vegetables of every kind. Fruit. Gelatins. Pastries. Puddings.

Rob looked at Collin, his eyes wide. "Okay, I lied. Maybe not this time." He grabbed a tray and began loading it down. When his tray could hold no more, Rob headed off to a corner with some friends.

Collin filled a plate and looked for a place to sit. The cafeteria had plenty of room. Many of the tables remained unoccupied.

Maybe now would be a good time to start her investigation of the camp. Who here might tell her what she needed to know? Or—more important—what she wanted to know?

Collin saw a man sitting alone toward the back. A man by no means—well, maybe by some means—okay…some might call him handsome. Sandy brown—bordering on red—hair, late twenties, early thirties…honest features.

What does the expression mean, anyhow? How can a nose be dishonest? Eyes, now, those can tell a tale. Except his head is down. Good thing. He might catch you staring.

Sort of. A little.

The man wore the garb of a maintenance worker. Collin vaguely remembered passing someone in a uniform earlier this evening. The bus. He unloaded the bus. He'd spoken to her. *And you walked right past him.*

Collin's eyes widened at the memory. Her heart sank.

Maybe he won't remember. Maybe he won't remember you. Maybe…

The man had a book propped up in front of his tray, reading as he ate. Collin felt embarrassed at the thought of walking up and saying, "Hi. I'm the rude woman who ignored you earlier. Can I join you now?"

Shameless much? Maybe he doesn't want company. Maybe he doesn't want your company. Maybe…

Collin growled, *Shut up!* She straightened her back and walked purposefully across the room, only to slow to a stop again as she neared his table. Campers rushed past her, determined on emptying as much of the buffet as possible. Collin dodged and weaved while she tried to make up her mind. She couldn't walk up to a perfect stranger and force herself on him, could she? Could she?

The man looked at her and smiled. The eyes did, indeed, tell a story.

Collin rebuked the coward inside. *You bet I can.* She advanced to the table, smiled, and asked, "Mind if I sit down?"

The man waved gallantly, moving his books aside. "Of course not. It took you long enough to make up your mind, though."

So he'd been watching her? Did he remember the bus? Collin demurred slightly at the challenge. "I promise I won't disturb you."

"Good. People tell me I'm disturbed enough as it is." He grinned.

Collin sat. She needed to take charge of this situation and fast. She extended her hand. "I'm Collin Walker."

The man reached out his hand but drew it back slightly. Collin noted his hands, though clean, bore the stains from oil, grease, and other lubricants of his trade. She reached out further and took his hand firmly. "Hi, I'm Collin Walker."

"Jeff Farrell." He pointed to the name on his shirt. "My reminder."

"I need something to remind me where I am, not who I am." *There are too many whos anyhow.*

Which we will not discuss now.

"Do you travel a lot?"

"More than I'd like but probably less than I should." She let Jeff chew on her statement while she bowed her head and gave thanks for her food.

When she looked up, the man wore a different look on his face, a look Collin couldn't read. Did she offend him? Better to find out now than later.

He smiled. "A woman who's not afraid to practice what she believes even in a crowd. You are a rare find."

Collin deflected the subject. She pointed to her plate. "I'm not sure what I've got here. What's good?"

"Everything Chef Michael fixes. He's a fantastic cook. Your kids will go home fat and happy—well, they will if we don't run the calories off them first."

Collin ducked her head. "We hope you do." She picked up one of the books sitting on the table. "What are you studying? Why are you studying? It's Friday night."

"Electrical wiring. So, I can make sure we have power Saturday morning." He looked at her. "You know anything about electrical wiring?"

"I know enough to call an electrician when I have a problem."

Jeff stared at her as if floored. He closed his eyes, lowered his head in disbelief, and slammed the book shut. A grin appeared and he let out a satisfied, "Yes!" He nodded to Collin. "Thank you. Thank you very much."

Lastly, he looked skyward. "And thank You!" He grinned. "No, I'm not nuts. I've been fighting for two days trying to solve this problem, and it's not mine. I need to call an expert." He laughed. "I get so wrapped up trying to do things on my own." He stopped, straightened, and turned sober. "I'm sure you've never experienced anything like that. You wouldn't know."

Collin waggled her head. "Of course not. Never. Not even once." She looked at the ceiling. "You have lightning rods on your roof?"

"No. Do we need them?"

"If I don't quit lying, you will. What kind of problem are you having?" An orange missiled from one side of the room to the other. Collin stood, glared at the offending parties, and yelled, "Knock it off! You're not at school."

A chorus of voices called, "Sorry, Ms. Walker." She sat back down. "Your problem?"

Jeff looked surprised. "You actually want to know?"

"I actually want to know."

Jeff settled back in his chair. "Okay, it started Wednesday when we lost power to the horse barn. We thought a breaker might have gone out, but they all tested good. The power came back on while we tried the lines themselves, which proved a great shock to all of us."

Collin smiled at the joke and sampled her food. She tried the tuna casserole first. It smelled and tasted like what she remembered from home in Fort Newton.

The smell cracked open the door on a gaping black hole. Memories came flooding back, ones she thought she'd closed years ago. Collin stared into the depths, feeling the familiar death grip on her awareness. *"You're useless! You're stupid! You're a waste of time! No one loves you. The world is better off without you. Don't come back. Don't ever come back..."*

Collin sat paralyzed. Unable to think, unable to move, unable to shut down the memories, she stared into the abyss of her past.

A roar of laughter from across the cafeteria startled Collin back to life. She realized she'd blacked out when Jeff finished his story, "And why we used the elephants."

Busted. She tried to cover anyhow. "Fascinating. I thought you used kangaroos." She looked Jeff in the eyes as if nothing happened.

He leaned forward and looked at her sideways. "Where did you go? I've never seen someone zone out so completely. I didn't mean to bore you, but you did ask."

She fumbled for an answer—or an explanation. "I'm sorry. It's not personal. Trust me." She smiled and shrugged. "It happens."

The man sat back in his chair. "Don't apologize. Teach me how to do it. I've got some professors I'd like to try it on. It would make their lectures a lot less boring. Or at least tolerable."

Collin gave him a half-smile. She followed his rabbit trail. "So you're in school? Where?"

He shrugged. "Grad school. Back in Oakton. Studying electrical engineering. But I think it's hopeless." He smiled. "And useless. All I need to know is to call the expert, right?"

"Right." She banished the shadows.

A raucous game of handball began across the way. Collin looked over to see if there were any other adults in the room. She saw Mr. Tremont accost the boys throwing the ball. Good. His turn to be monitor. Jeers rewarded his confiscation of the toy. Several of the diners headed out of the room, back to the top floor. Collin noted Rob wasn't with them.

Investigate the camp. Investigate the camp. "Are you from around here?"

"No. I commute from Oakton. I work the challenge camps and set up and tear down for the handicap sessions we offer in the late fall. I love to watch what this place can do for a kid."

"Camp Grace isn't just for kids?"

"We do about four challenge camps for the inner city crowd in the summer. Spring and fall, we're a regular for-hire camp. Winter, we're a ski resort."

"It must keep you busy."

"It does." He looked at her tray. "You stopped eating."

Collin's appetite vanished. She pushed her tray away. "I'm done."

Jeff frowned. "You can't be done. You never even started."

Collin ignored the comment, though his concern interested her. She changed the subject. "What do you do when you're not at camp and you're not in school? Isn't it tough on your family with you gone all the time?"

One corner of Jeff's smile lifted. "You mean like a wife-and-child-kind of family? Is that what you're asking?"

Collin shrugged. "Not exactly. But are you?"

"Am I what?"

"Married?"

"Would it make a difference?"

Collin said sharply—more sharply than she intended—"Yes."

"Good. It should. No, I'm not. No children, either. And I hope that makes a difference, too."

The man intrigued her. She couldn't read him at all except for his eyes. And she dare not look there too long, nor too deep. "It does." She challenged, "It means you at least have the decency to consider someone else before subjecting them to your harebrained lifestyle."

Jeff grinned. "*Touché*. It's not forever. One day I hope to work here full time. But now, economics play a big part in the decision. I have commitments in Oakton."

"Like what?"

"You are nosy, aren't you?"

"I'm a counselor. It's what we do. We ask questions. We make observations. We evaluate. We dig around, we…" Warning bells clanged in her head. Too much truth for this weekend. Collin sat up straighter and tried to smile.

Jeff rolled his eyes. "My turn to ask questions. I know you're a counselor. I know you're a very dedicated counselor because you're either using your vacation time to be here, or taking the week off without pay, which would mean you're a very wealthy counselor, and you wouldn't be in this line of work unless you really, really loved kids. In which case, you'd be the one bankrolling this trip."

Collin started to correct the man's impressions of her, but he continued without a breath. "Do you have any family? Meaning besides the obligatory mother, father, siblings, and yes, I'm asking specifically, are you married? I see no ring or ring shadow, but that doesn't mean what it used to. Married women don't wear rings, and unmarried women have them on every finger. How's a guy supposed to know the difference?"

Collin chuckled. "Did you have a question in there?"

"Several. One, are you married? Two, do you have a family? Three, what do you do to enjoy yourself?"

"One, no. Two, no. Three…um…I am enjoying myself."

"You are?"

Someone must have announced closing. Campers jumped up and made a mad rush to empty the buffet line of as much food as they could carry. Collin nodded. "Yes, I am. It's been a while since I've conversed with someone older than seventeen. Not on this level anyhow."

Jeff looked around. "What, down in the basement?"

Collin tapped the table lightly. "Stop before you hurt yourself. You know what I mean."

Jeff spread his hands in acquiescence. "Okay."

Collin went back on the offensive. "When you're not in school, and you're not up here, what do you do for fun?"

"I'm a paramedic."

Collin grew solemn. "Oh, *this* is the fun stuff."

His eyes softened. "This is the fun stuff. It's not always intense, and I love what I do. But coming here gives me a break."

The maintenance worker stretched. "It also gives me a break from my dad. I manage some properties for him, and he's death on details."

Collin stomped the door to the black hole. *No memories. Not now.* "I see. How long—"

Rob sauntered up to the table with his "I be cool" act. But Collin read the excitement under the surface. At least him, she could still decipher. "Yes?"

"A bunch of us is gonna walk to the canyon floor to see the river. You want to come, caseworker lady?"

Collin waved him off. "No, Rob. You go. I'd slow you down, seeing as you're always telling me I'm 'old folk,' you know."

Jeff supported Rob. "It's beautiful. You ought to go."

Collin continued to refuse. "Maybe later."

Rob protested, "Aw, come on, caseworker lady. I promise, ain't none of us gonna fall in." The boy bounced on the toes of his shoes.

Jeff added, "The trail's well marked, and there's a turn out with benches. We keep it lit in the evenings. It's a great spot."

Collin studied the maintenance man. Why would he dismiss her so soon? Seen what he wanted, and she'd failed the test? What did she say this time?

Jeff stood. "I'll be here all week. I'd like it if we could talk again." He grinned. "Maybe you can explain about the kangaroos." He carried both his and Collin's tray to the counter and deposited them.

Somewhat encouraged, Collin nodded. "I hope so." She looked at Rob. "Okay, man. Do you know how to get there? More important, do you know how to get back?" Collin stood and pushed in her chair.

Rob laughed. "Lady, have I ever got lost?"

Collin glared. "Not the question. You've got me lost plenty of times telling me how to get someplace to pick you up or drop you off. I refuse to be a den mate with some grizzly because you can't remember the way home."

Rob chuckled. "Ain't no grizzlies in West Virginia."

"How do you know?"

"I learnt it in school."

Collin put a hand on her heart. "You learned it in school? You mean they taught you something you remembered? Will wonders never cease?"

Rob pulled her arm. "Yeah, yeah, I know. So maybe it wasn't all a waste of time. Maybe some stuff stuck. Let's go."

Collin waved at Jeff as Rob dragged her off. "I hope I see you around, Jeff."

As Rob pulled Collin out of earshot, she heard his assuring, "You will."

~

As ten kids—and one counselor—hiked ever downward toward the riverbank, Collin's fear grew. Even the jostling and jesting of the group couldn't keep the shadows at bay.

Finally, she reached her breaking—and braking—point. Collin stopped as they neared the lookout. They were still maybe fifty yards from where the river would be visible. Close enough to feel the throbbing pulse in her being, but not close enough to feel the spray in her face. On her face. Over her face...

Collin told Rob, "You guys go on. I'll wait here."

Rob looked at her, confused. "What? Why?"

"I got my reasons. You young guns forget what goes down easy goes back up exponentially harder. I'll rest up here and beat you all back up the hill. Go on."

She saw disappointment in his eyes. But he put on his tough-guy facade. "Suit yourself. We be back later."

Collin sighed as he turned and followed the crowd. She needed to come up with an explanation. One near enough to the truth so it wouldn't be a lie, but dull enough to keep anyone from asking questions. Collin sat back against a tree, set her mind on reviewing praise hymns she knew. It would occupy the time—and her brain—until the kids returned.

Half an hour later, a subdued group returned. Collin guessed the reason but decided to make them put it into words to help crystallize the experience. She asked, "How was it, Luke?"

The ten-year-old shook his head. "I never seen anything like it.

Nothing. It's so…so…" He faltered.

Jeshua bailed him out. "So powerful. So big. Only running water I've ever seen comes out in the tub. I didn't know there could be something so…"

As the young teen ran out of words, twelve-year-old Awana picked up the torch. "Yeah, I know what you mean. I've seen rivers on those nature shows my folks make me watch." She grimaced. "But seeing it on a little screen doesn't give you any idea how…"

No one filled in the blank. No one could. Collin understood their feelings. "And this is only the first night. What else do you think they have out here?"

Silence met her, as ten teens and teen wannabes considered the possibilities ahead. Finally, someone—Collin couldn't be sure who—whispered, "Wow."

Suddenly someone else, equally anonymous, quipped, "Hey, I can say it backward! Wow." He dragged the word out for emphasis.

Several someones slugged the jokester, who ran off, jeering at his jury. Swift pursuit followed and swiftly halted, as the steepness of the hill overcame even their youthful exuberance. A mid-range walk became the gait of choice and talking gave way to simply breathing.

As the group returned to the lodge, Rob pulled Collin aside. "Caseworker lady, you mind not getting whooped in hoops tonight? It ain't gonna spoil your day or nothing, will it?"

"Why, Rob?"

"I don't know." Collin rarely saw Rob this subdued or contemplative. "I think I want to be alone for a while. Be alone and jus' think. Something 'bout the river jus' make me wanna think."

Collin nodded. "I understand." She let out a somewhat shaky breath. "Tomorrow night."

They came to the parting of the sexes: boys' rooms to the left, girls' rooms to the right, with a staffed entry hall between them. Collin stopped, turned, and faced Rob. "You okay, bro?"

He nodded. "Yeah. It's everything out there is so…so…" Collin waited for him to get his thought out. He apparently couldn't find the words any more than the other teens, so finished lamely, "…so big, I guess. I mean, city buildings is big, but man built them. I could build one of them. But the trees and the river, all of it…it's huge, and it got that way without me being here, without no man being here helping it or telling it what to do. Like we don't even matter or nothing."

Collin ached to hug the boy but knew better than to cross forbidden territory. "You matter, Rob. More than you know, you matter. Goodnight, bro. Get some sleep." *At least one of us should.*

"Night, caseworker lady."

The two parted company and went to their respective rooms. Collin checked on her two charges, who lay in the same bed. She set an eleven-p.m. curfew on giggling and a midnight cut-off on talking. Probably a waste of time; the girls would be asleep within the hour anyhow.

Collin went back to her room. She debated whether to shower now or in the morning. The six-a.m. alarm came early. But the thought of running water cascading over her head added more fuel to an already-glowing ember she meant to extinguish. Collin changed into her nightshirt, took her Bible from her backpack, and settled into bed. She muttered, "Numbers. Genealogies. If those can't put me to sleep, nothing can." She looked at the first page of the chapter. "I hope."

Outside the windows, the heartbeat of the river pulsed along.

ABOUT THE AUTHOR

Colleen K. Snyder has always had a passion for writing. She authored two previously published books: *Journey to Amanah: The Beginning* and *Return to Tebel-Ayr: The Journey Continues* (B&H Publishing). She lives on a "ranchette" in California and is the juniorest ranch hand. She serves on her church prayer team, writes the weekly prayer letter, and exercises a ministry of intercessory prayer. She has worked as a factory line worker, pharmacy technician, USAF missile systems analyst, janitor, nanny, teacher, accounting manager and anything else the Lord required. Her son, Bear and his wife Krystal, their two daughters, Mara and Kaylynn, and her daughter Katie all live in Ohio.

Colleen's story is for His glory, always.

Connect with her on Facebook at Colleen K. Snyder, Author and on her website colleensnyderauthor.com.

www.ingramcontent.com/pod-product-compliance
Lightning Source LLC
Chambersburg PA
CBHW061215210726
48294CB00006B/1845